Fen Runners

Also by John Gordon

The Giant Under the Snow

Fen Runners

John Gordon

Chapter head illustrations by Gary Blythe

Orion
Children's Books

First published in Great Britain in 2009
by Orion Children's Books
a division of the Orion Publishing Group Ltd
Orion House
5 Upper St Martin's Lane
London WC2H 9EA
An Hachette Livre UK Company

1 3 5 7 9 10 8 6 4 2

A catalogue record for this book is available from the British Library

ISBN 978 1 84255 684 9

Typeset by Input Data Services Ltd, Bridgwater Somerset

Printed in Great Britain by CPI Antony Rowe, Chippenham, Wiltshire

www.orionbooks.co.uk

For Sylvia

CONTENTS

ONE

DUTCHMAN'S CUT

They stood with their toes curled over the edge of the bridge and looked briefly into the distance. Beneath them the waters of Dutchman's Cut sliced the landscape in a dead straight line from horizon to horizon and there was no one within miles to see them. There were no words. One of the boys raised his eyebrows, the other dipped his head and they dived together.

Kit Mallion felt the cut of the water as he left the last of the summer overhead and swam down until the long fronds of water weed caressed his belly and sides. Somewhere, already lost in the peat-brown water, Joe French was forcing his way through the same cool forest. He was the better swimmer and likely to stay under longer but, this time, Kit was going to surprise him.

Above them the ripples of their plunge had fled to the grassy banks and died. Kit kicked and went deeper until his fingers dug into the silt at the bottom and he clung to the roots of the weed to fight the buoyancy that was pushing him upwards.

Lungs don't burst. He was aware of that. They try to implode, sucking in cool water, and already he was fighting off that first deadly gulp. Both hands were deep in the silt and he lay in the water counting the seconds as his body slowly rotated until he hung head-down, anchored to the bottom of the channel. By now Joe must have swum up for air.

Time to go. He slipped one hand free and tugged with the other, but he had twisted a root around his wrist and it did not budge. He twisted again, narrowing his fingers, but the root bit deeper and held. He was tethered to the silt. Panic made him bend his knees as if to run but his toes pressed on nothing firmer than water and he was writhing in the grip of a nightmare going nowhere ... nowhere ... until, in the final fatal agony, he felt the root loosening its own grip in the mud and he rose to thrash on the surface, open his mouth and claim back his life.

Joe's voice, laughing. 'Where do you think you've been all this time?'

'Drowning.' He was coughing, keeping his chin clear of the water. 'But I won.' The weed was still around his wrist, a clump of black roots that clung to him until he fought his way to the bank and flung the mass on to the grass.

Joe, plump as a seal, his hair streaked over his eyes, gazed at him from the water and asked, 'What've you got there?'

'Mud.'

'There's a lump of metal in it.'

'Bit of an old bike.' Kit hardly looked at it. Something had cut his finger, but to shed the clutch of the roots was all that mattered.

Joe swam to the bank. He was interested. 'It still shines a bit,' he said, and then his imagination took over. 'It could be a blade.' He touched it. 'I reckon it *is* a blade. I know what it is . . . it's a sword!'

'Far too short.' Kit knew that even if he had dragged up a scrap of rotting wood Joe would believe it to be the plank of a causeway made by the ancient fenmen who had once lived their secret lives here, among the marshy reed beds that had once covered the whole flat landscape. So a bit of old metal had to be a weapon.

3

'And,' Kit said aloud, 'it's bent at one end and far too blunt.' From the clump of weed he picked out a fragment of what seemed to be oyster shell. One side of it shone like mother-of-pearl and it had a sharp edge. 'That's what cut me.'

'No,' Joe persisted. 'That blade could still be a dagger.'

'It's a bit of an old kitchen cabinet.' Kit tossed it higher up the bank.

The sun was high but autumn was in the air and they shivered as they rubbed their arms and legs to dry off. They had no towels or swimming trunks, but this far out in the fens there was no one to see them, and the endless smooth water of Dutchman's Cut had been a temptation they could not resist.

Joe soon stopped shivering, but he saw that Kit's limbs were still jerking with cold. 'You shouldn't be so skinny,' he said, 'but I'm fairly glad you didn't drown.'

'Thanks. If I don't come up next time you can have my bike.'

They had reached this spot only by hard pedalling along earth tracks between the fields, and Cottle's Bridge had been a good place to rest. It was not a picturesque bridge; it was no more than a single flat span used by farm tractors, and there had been no one working on the land when they had stripped and plunged. Kit glanced at their bikes lying in the grass.

Other bikes had been found like that after their owners had gone missing only to be found when Dutchman's Cut had been dredged. He had been close to following those missing owners through the same dark doorway. He shivered and turned away and it was only then, from the corner of his eye, that he saw they were not alone. A figure was standing on Cottle's Bridge, looking at them.

Kit's jeans clung to his wet skin as he tried to haul them up and anger overcame his shock. He turned to Joe and spoke under his breath. 'Tell him to go away.'

'Tell him yourself.' Joe's shirt was stuck to his chest.

But neither spoke. They were almost dressed, their bikes were near at hand and in a few moments they could be speeding away along the track at the top of the bank. Kit, suddenly confident, shouted up at the man, 'What's wrong with you? We haven't done anything we shouldn't. Go away!'

That encouraged Joe. 'Yes,' he shouted, 'push off!'

They could see there was no danger. The man was not large, his shoulders were hunched, and he looked old. But he did not budge, and when he spoke his voice was no more than a murmur. 'What you got there?' he said and pointed to the clump of weed on the bank.

'Nothing to do with you,' Joe retorted.

'Bring it to me.'

'No!' Joe was not obeying orders, and he turned to Kit. 'Chuck it back in the cut and we'll get away.' They were dressed and ready.

But Kit suddenly did not want to throw away something he had struggled to bring to the bank. 'He's harmless,' he muttered. 'He might as well see it.' He pulled the rusty metal free of the weed and, with Joe grumbling behind him, he pushed his bike up the slope.

They had nothing to fear. The man was very little taller than themselves, and although he was much broader they saw that some of his width was due to the tattered clothes he wore. His size was bulked out by rags over rags, every ancient garment worn to little more than a mesh of holes but never discarded, never washed, merely laid mesh over mesh until he was a warm, mouldering heap of brown and grey. On top was a round head under a sad, greasy cap in the shadow of which two liquid eyes looked out.

'I seen a lot o' things throwed in that water,' he muttered, 'and some of 'em have been good stuff . . . valuable things . . . worth a bit.'

Joe, keeping a straight face, asked, 'Is that where you found your cap, Mr Cottle?'

'No.' The ragged man ignored the name Joe had given him and answered seriously. 'I bought it off of a stall on the market – same place as you got your bike, by the look of it.'

'I never . . .' Then Joe remembered that his machine came second-hand from an alleyway behind the market place. But that was in town, seven miles away, where he lived. He had never seen this ambling heap anywhere, and he could hardly have missed the ragged man from Cottle's Bridge.

Kit grinned. The old man was obviously not so stupid as to think a scrap of old iron was valuable, but perhaps he had glimpsed the rainbow colours of the oyster shell. It was roughly circular and Kit held it out for him to see. The man, however, shook his head.

'I couldn't hold it, young 'un – me hands is too cloudy-cold.'

'What do you mean . . . cloudy-cold?' Kit turned slightly to look at Joe, but Joe was expressionless.

'Me hands is too cloudy-cold – they won't hold nothin'.'

'Not even this magnificent sword blade?' Kit, to get a smile from Joe, held out the scrap iron as if he was a knight handing it to his king but, midway through the flourish, he paused because Joe did not seem to be watching. The joke had fallen flat. Joe's face was expressionless, and the old man was annoyed. 'You want to put that away,' he grunted. 'That ain't no sword.'

Joe came to life. 'What is it, then?'

'That's a pattern, that's what that is.'

'Pattern of what?'

'You'll find out soon enough.'

'Why not now?'

The ragged man ignored Joe's question and was gazing down into the water. 'You wouldn't want to be in that deep old cut now,' he said, 'not with that thing down there.'

The water was as blank as a window in an empty house but as they watched they saw something move in the emptiness. A pale shape came up from the depths, elongated itself as it neared the surface, slid by without a ripple, and vanished.

'What's that!' Joe could hardly breathe.

'People reckon there's a big old jack pike down there – and you only see him when he turns his belly up like he's doing now.'

Down there, where they had been swimming with the fingers of water weed stroking their skin, something was again sliding by. Bigger than a pike. As long as a man . . . longer, and as it again came near the bank its flank of silver-grey broke the surface and pushed against the grass at the water's edge.

It sank, and Kit forced himself to raise his eyes to the ragged man. But, unnoticed, the man had already shuffled to the far end of the bridge and was moving further away.

It was Joe's laugh that made Kit turn towards him.

'Not even a fish!' Joe raised his eyes from where the shape was again dissolving into the water and pointed at the sky. A few high clouds were swimming across the blue and it was their pale reflections that were trapped in the water and no silvery bulk was about to haul itself out of Dutchman's Cut.

Kit had little to say on the ride back to town. The ragged man was simply Old Cottle now and they laughed about him, but the pause in the air and then the shape in the water had affected Kit more than anything seemed to have worried Joe, and now the damp hair on his neck made him shudder.

'You're cold,' said Joe. 'Come and have some tea with us.' He lived in town, but when they got there Kit did not feel sociable enough and he still had to go to his village, so instead they took a stroll around the market place. The square cupped enough autumn sunshine to warm their bones and they were idly looking into a shop window that held no interest for them when a girl came hurriedly out of the doorway and caught Kit off-balance. The day's mishaps had not yet ended.

'Sorry,' he said, although it was not his fault and, seeing a man half hidden in the doorway directly

9

behind her and thinking it must be her father, he smiled and apologised again. At this the girl frowned suddenly, darkening her already dark eyes and pulling down the corners of her mouth.

Joe, watching him stagger into trouble, was amused, and it was his laugh that prevented the girl saying anything as she glanced back into the doorway and then again at Kit. There was an awkward moment before Joe tugged his arm and they walked on.

'Saved you that time,' said Joe. 'She was getting pretty angry.'

Pretty anyway, Kit almost said, but thought better of it. 'She was with her father ... so I couldn't say much to her, could I?'

'I didn't see anyone with her.'

'Well, just look.' Kit was pointing as the two figures turned a corner and went out of sight.

Joe was laughing. 'You've got water on the brain, just like Old Cottle out in there in the fens.'

It was not Kit's best day.

TWO

THE BACK OF BEYOND

'What have you got there?'

Kit did not have to look up. There were only two houses in the lane where he lived and it was so hidden away from the rest of the village that it was simply known as the Back of Beyond. He knew his neighbour's voice.

'You look cold,' said Mrs Strickland. Autumn had passed and winter had come. There was frost on the grass of the rutted lane, and Kit's mood was as chilly as the weather.

'I'm freezing,' he agreed. He had his bike upside

down on the path, and Mrs Strickland was looking over the gate between the two gardens.

'You poor chap.' She had been retired many years but she could not keep the teacher out of her voice. 'Can I fetch a cup of tea to warm you up?' she added kindly.

'No, thank you, Mrs Strickland.' She meant well, and she wasn't to blame for his bike being out of commission on a Saturday morning when he could have been cycling into town to see Joe.

'Well, may I ask again what that instrument is you are using?'

He held it up. 'Just a tyre lever. I've got a puncture.'

'No, Kit.' She was laughing. 'That's no tyre lever.'

'I know,' he agreed. 'It's just a bit of scrap iron that's been lying around in the garden shed for ages.'

Again she disagreed. 'I don't think it's scrap at all.'

'Well,' he looked at it, 'maybe not.' He was not about to embarrass himself by telling her that two months ago he had dived to the bottom of Dutchman's Cut and this was all he had brought up ... but she saved him the trouble of saying anything.

He heard her say, 'It's a pattern,' and his mind jumped immediately to the ragged man on the bridge. Old Cottle had talked about a pattern as if the rusted metal was the key to some deep mystery.

'Someone else told me that,' he admitted.

'Was there only the one in your garden shed?' she asked.

'Yes,' he said, 'Should there have been more?'

She was amused. 'Well, they always come in pairs, don't they?'

'Patterns do?' His face was blank. 'Nobody's ever told me that.'

She was laughing again. 'I'm not talking about patt-*erns*,' she said carefully. 'I'm talking about patt-*ens* – ice skates. Pattens is the fen word for ice skates.'

And then he remembered. '*Fen runners*, you mean!' He looked again at his tyre lever and now, with its curved end, it seemed more elegant ... it was a strip of steel made to skim over ice.

'And it fitted into a piece of wood which you strapped on your boot,' said Mrs Strickland. 'I skated on lovely fen runners when I was a young woman – but fancy you, a fen boy, not knowing what it was. And why is there only one?'

'Because I found it at the bottom of Dutchman's Cut.'

'Swimming?' she asked and, when he nodded, she added, 'I don't think I want to know about that.'

But she listened when he told her of diving to the bottom of the channel and hauling up the blade with a clump of weed although, as she listened, she pinched in her lips until her face was as severe as her name. Then she said, 'Didn't you two boys, swimming out there alone ... didn't you realise how dangerous it was?'

'Well I'm not going looking for the other one.' He held up the blade. 'Not in this weather.'

She did not smile. 'Where exactly did you find it?'

'We were diving off Cottle's Bridge ...' He was about to say more, but she drew in her breath and repeated, 'Cottle's Bridge?'

He nodded reluctantly, expecting more criticism, but her expression had changed completely and she was looking at him with bright eyes and telling him, 'Then I know to whom this belongs!' She took the blade, gripped it with both hands and cried, 'Tom Townsend – and I saw him lose it!'

She handed it back to Kit, expecting him to share in her excitement, but his fingers seemed to freeze to the metal as if he was once more tied to it by the water weed that had held him to the bottom of Dutchman's Cut. He even, for a long moment, felt himself suffocating like the young man who had been wearing the skate when Mrs Strickland saw him plunge through the ice. And that was long ago.

'Did he drown?' The words came out even though he felt he himself was still fighting for breath.

'Tom Townsend?' Mrs Strickland was laughing. 'No, not Tom – he's still alive, the young rascal.'

Hardly young now if he was Mrs Strickland's age.

'There was a big freeze that year and the skating was wonderful,' she continued. 'We would go for miles . . . and we went too far out along Dutchman's Cut because it was getting dark before we realised it was time to head for home. Tom was far ahead of us when he got to Cottle's Bridge and he decided he'd wait for us there.

'We saw him cutting circles under the bridge and I knew . . . I just *knew* that something would go wrong, because you know how wet the ice sometimes is under a bridge . . . well it was weak, and we suddenly saw him staggering all over the place and a great shadow seemed to loom up out of the water . . .'

'Shadow?' Kit forced her to pause. The memory of a great fish pushing into the grass at the waterside filled his mind. 'What did it look like?'

'I thought it was human.' She was laughing. 'I thought he was dancing with someone who, even in that light, seemed to be wearing a silvery garment of some sort . . . but it wasn't *human*, of course.' She paused, and Kit ceased to breathe. 'It was just a great slab of ice that tilted up . . . and poor Tom went down, straight into the water.'

'And that was all?'

'Isn't that enough for you?' She was laughing again. 'It was quite enough for poor Tom – because he cut his hand quite badly in the process.'

Kit held back from saying the same had happened to him. 'How did he get out?' he asked.

'My friend and I – there were just the two of us – we lay down flat to spread our weight but we were having great trouble and I could tell that Tom was getting really scared, but then a man came along and we got Tom to the bank. We were thankful, I can tell you, but this man simply wandered away and we never saw him again.'

'And you were still miles away from the village,' Kit said.

'*And* poor Tom had only one skate and was wet to the skin. It took a long time to get back here.'

Kit had never heard of Tom Townsend. 'Does he still live in the village?' he asked.

She looked at him shrewdly. 'If you mean – is he still alive? Yes, he is, and he lives in Welbeck and as you go to school there I'm surprised you've never heard of him.'

Mrs Strickland saw Kit shrug, but she smiled. 'Mr Townsend may mean nothing to you, Kit, and I haven't seen him for years, but I believe he's quite important in Welbeck.' She handed the blade back to Kit. 'He'd just love to know this has been found, but as he made such a fool of himself at the time, and I saw it happen, I don't think I'm the one to tell him.'

THREE

SHADOWS

She knew nothing about him. Not even the colour of his hair. In the shop doorway, when they bumped into each other, his hair had been wet and smooth and must have seemed darker than it really was – but not ginger like the boy who was with him. She knew the ginger one by sight but had no memory of the stranger. There were many things that passed her by these days, but not the one thing that mattered. That was with her almost all the time, but no one could understand. They thought it was her imagination running wild and she would 'get over it' in time.

But that boy was different. He understood something. She was sure of it.

'Jenny!' Her mother's voice from downstairs. 'Breakfast!'

She went to the door of her tiny room and looked down the stairwell to her mother in the hall three storeys below. 'I'm almost ready.'

From the landing she could hear the murmur of an occasional car making its way round the Crescent, but her room at the back of the narrow old house was silent. Across the rooftops she could see her own school not far from the centre of town. She need not hurry. It was only a short walk away. The ginger boy went to school on the other side of the river. The fair boy would go there with him, she was sure. But he wasn't a town boy. She would have seen him more often if he lived in Welbeck.

There was a cold mist over the fens but Kit was warm in the kitchen. He looked out into the lane. The ruts in the Back of Beyond were like miniature mountain ranges topped with a white crust of ice and he decided that, on the whole, he preferred to take the bus to school.

'I'll need my fare,' he said.

'I thought you'd mended your puncture.' His mother was more concerned with getting herself ready for work behind the post office counter in the village.

'I was interrupted,' he said. 'I don't think I mended it properly.' It was so feeble an excuse that he winced, but she had already handed him the money and was standing at the door to lock it behind them. His father had already driven off on his rounds as a farm agent.

Three flights of stairs were not exactly a spiral, but as she went down Jenny allowed herself to feel like a bird launching itself from a high rooftop. Nothing followed her. Not this time.

'How are you this morning, Jenny love?' Her mother tried but could never hide the anxiety in her eyes.

'There's nothing to worry about, Mum.' She paused to make her mother look at her. 'There's nothing ... nothing at all.' No need for more words between them. No need for her mother to look for the shadows behind Jenny's back that only Jenny could ever see.

'You'll need a good breakfast.' Her mother made herself busy at the table. 'It's cold outside.'

'It must have been freezing when Dad got up – and pitch black.'

'Don't worry about your father – he's more than warm enough.'

'All those ovens!' Jenny had often visited the bakery

hidden away in the jumble of streets behind the market place. 'Who'd be a pastry cook!'

'He would. It's what he's always wanted.'

Jenny nodded. 'Except ...' she began, and left a gap in the air.

Her mother sighed. 'We all know that things were once a lot better, Jenny, but no one's to blame for that.'

Jenny had hardly touched her breakfast. 'But I'm no help, am I?'

Her mother came closer. 'You and your father,' she said quietly. 'You're both the same. You take it all on your own shoulders – but there's no one to blame for his old place having to close down and him having to find a new job. No one.'

'But I didn't help,' said Jenny. She knew she had been a worry to him with her nightmares that still, sometimes, haunted her even in daylight.

'You are both too imaginative.'

It was true. Neither she nor her father felt comfortable whenever they passed the place where he had worked until it closed down. It had been known simply as the Cake Shop because that was what it was on the ground floor, but above it was the restaurant that she knew had been famous in its day. The whole building, however, had been locked up and deserted for years. Jenny had never known why but she, like her father, always felt uncomfortable as they walked by.

Jenny blamed herself. She was the one who had the nightmares and often saw things that no one else could see. She was the one who could not even use a mobile phone because of the screeching it always made inside her head. She guessed that her father had once been the same but he would never admit it. Perhaps it was something she could put behind her, as he had done. In the meantime her mother worried.

Jenny suddenly stood up. 'I think it's all over,' she said. 'No shadows today. Nothing.'

Her mother looked keenly at her, wanting to believe.

'I haven't seen anything for ages. They've never done me any harm ... why should I care about *anything*?' But she could not prevent a shudder, like a dog after a plunge.

It was crowded on the bus. Mist lay across the fens but there was enough pale sunshine to show the shadow of the bus ripple along the roadside ditch like a runner brushing through the reeds.

Someone said, 'I seen a skim of ice along Winter Wash when I come through this morning.' The Wash was bare grassland between the banks of two drainage channels that stretched for miles in a dead straight line. Cattle grazed there in summer but in winter the land was allowed to flood, and water birds flocked there. 'All them swans is going to have a hard time if a freeze come.'

Another voice said, 'Old Babs Horn would have liked it.' Babs was a famous skater of long ago. 'I expect his ghost is gettin' ready for it right now.'

There was a laugh and Kit was tempted to show that he was carrying the blade of an old fen runner that had a strange history, but he thought better of it. At least hearing them talk put an end to his doubts about handing it back to Mr Townsend and maybe reminding him of a time he would rather forget. If there was going to be a freeze, Mr Townsend may even enjoy the memory of skating long ago and take to the ice again.

Such thoughts dwindled when Kit crossed the town's main bridge to walk to school. The surging brown flood of the river beneath him would never freeze, and the same was almost certainly true of the smooth fen waterways. He could barely remember the last time there had been ice that would bear his weight.

And Joe looked blankly at him when he said, 'I've brought the blade.'

'What blade?'

It was only then that Kit realised his mind had been

so full of Mrs Strickland's story of the lost skate that he had neglected to pass it on to Joe.

But Joe, when he heard about it, was full of doubt. 'If you believe that,' he said, 'you'll believe anything.'

'I thought you'd come with me when I gave it back to Mr Townsend.'

Joe frowned. 'You mean the Tom Townsend who lives in Wilberforce Avenue?'

'That's the address she gave me.'

'I suppose you know who he is?' Joe's jaw was set and he frowned.

Kit shrugged. 'Just a man.'

'Just a man who sacked my uncle!' Joe wanted to lash out. 'He hadn't done anything wrong – nobody had – but a few little things troubled *Mister* Tom Townsend and lots of people lost their jobs – including my uncle!'

Joe was speaking for his family. He had heard a lot of talk, but now Kit hoped to calm him. 'I just thought,' he said quietly, 'that we could duck out of school at lunchtime and go to see him. I don't know where Wilberforce Avenue is.'

That was too feeble to influence Joe. 'It's too far,' he said. 'We'd never make it in time.'

'After school?'

Joe shook his head. 'That man Townsend still has a shop in Market Street. If you really want to give him his skate you could try shoving it through the letterbox.'

The sky was darkening and the town seemed to have shut down early as Kit put school behind him and walked along the riverside alone. The four lamps at the corners of the bridge seemed to half close their eyes against the wind that was helping the brown water push its way to the sea, and when he got to the market square it was bleak and empty. He had time to waste before his bus so he strolled as far as Market Street to find the Townsend shop. Perhaps he could hand the skate blade over the counter and leave the shop staff to explain it to their employer. Then he could forget it and make his peace with Joe.

But there was no shop. He walked the street twice, looking up at the nameboards, but there was nothing with the name of Townsend, and soon it would be too late. Lights in shop windows were going out, and the pavements were already deserted.

There was no one to take notice of a loiterer. The street was gloomy but he took his time and was almost at the end where Market Street joined the deeper shadows of the Crescent when he stopped in front of premises that he had hardly bothered to examine. The building was now unoccupied and so grimy and run-down it was almost derelict. A metal grille covered its front window and an iron gate guarded its entrance. Then he saw the letterbox bolted to the gate and from the litter inside the doorway it was obvious it had not been used for years. Was this where he had been advised to leave the blade for Mr Townsend to see?

He stepped back to read the nameboard and discovered he was standing in front of the Cake Shop Café, and under the title he could just make out the words *Thos. Townsend proprietor.*

'Thanks, Joe!' he said. If he had left the blade here it would not have been seen for years.

In the gloom of the street he stepped forward to peer through the grille over the window. He could just make out white shelves, cabinets, a counter with an old cash register. He was reaching through the grille to clear a patch in the grime when he thought he saw a dim shape moving inside the shop. He pulled his hand away. He was mistaken. The shop was empty except for shadows, and the shadows were motionless.

He put his head closer to the grille to try to peer deeper into the shop, but found it impossible. He pressed closer to the glass . . . and found himself almost face to face with a tall figure stooping to look out.

FOUR

THE CAROL SINGER

'Just you watch what you get up to.' The warning came from Kit's mother as she got into the car. She had begun the annoying habit when Mrs Strickland, greatly amused by the discovery of the skate, had told her of his plunge into Dutchman's Cut.

'I might be a bit late getting back,' he said. It was Saturday and he allowed her to believe he was to spend the day with Joe. She did not have to know that Joe was visiting cousins and would not be there.

His father could also be embarrassing. He winked

and said, 'Don't let her keep you in town too long –
whoever she is.'

'There is no *her*!'

'Tough.'

As the car crunched across the gravel they grimaced
at each other. This time Kit meant it even though he
knew that most of his anger was directed at himself.
In the last few days he had more than once made
himself peer into the empty cake shop and he had
seen nothing to be afraid of – he must have been
scared by his own reflection. But now ... he took a
deep breath ... but now he was to ride into town to
confront the grim café owner and remind him of an
undignified incident in his past. Wishing that he had
never allowed Mrs Strickland to catch a glimpse of
the skate blade, Kit wrapped it in a piece of cloth and
put it in his backpack.

A cold breeze pressed against him as he left the
Back of Beyond, as if warning him to go no further,
and it was still in his face as he rode into town. It
died away only when, following Joe's instructions, he
turned into Wilberforce Avenue. It was broad and
tree-lined and so silent that he found himself riding
slowly to lessen the whisper of his wheels. Number 14
had its own forest of shrubs and a winding path
that took him to a tall, black-painted front door that
gleamed like a polished funeral car.

'Yes?'

The voice was harsh and came at him as the door swung open even before his hand had reached the bell-pull. He took a half-step back as a bald head leaned out and the voice rapped, 'If you are who I think you are . . .' The man paused, his glasses dangling on a cord around his neck, before he barked, '. . . just one verse of *Hark, the herald angels* and don't tell your friends or they'll all be round.'

The man's bald head gleamed as harshly as the door and a frown cut a deep shadow between his eyes. 'Well, start up the band,' he ordered, 'or you don't get a penny.'

'But . . .' Kit struggled to stand up to him, 'it's three weeks to Christmas.'

'I know it is. You get earlier every year.'

'But I'm not . . .' He wanted to say he wasn't anything like a doorstep carol singer when the man realised his mistake.

'Oh-oh,' he said, 'you're the newspaper boyo . . . how much is it this week?'

The man had somehow managed to make Kit feel much younger than he was, so that it seemed very childlike when he held out the strip of metal wrapped in cloth and said, 'I brought you this.'

It was only then that the lines in the man's long

face lost some of their anger. 'Oh,' he said. 'How much do I owe you?'

'Nothing. It's something you lost.'

'Did I . . . ?'

Kit braced himself. Perhaps he was speaking to the wrong man.

'I don't recall losing anything . . .' the man began, but a woman's voice called out, 'Is that him?'

'Maybe,' he said uncertainly, but then his wife was beside him.

'Tom Townsend,' she said, 'you're a fool. This is not the boiler man. He hasn't got a bag of tools, and he's far too young. . . he's going to sing us a carol.'

It took many words but in the end they laughed at themselves for mistaking Kit for the boiler man and invited him in, and by the time they had talked themselves through the hall and into a sitting room at the back of the house it had dawned on the old couple that Kit had come to restore something they had lost long ago.

Kit unwrapped the blade and held it out, expecting Tom Townsend to take it but, at his first glimpse of the metal, the old man withdrew his hand and left it to his wife to hold the blade.

'My word, won't that be useful!' she exclaimed, but instantly had to ask, 'What is it, er . . .' and raised her eyebrows at him seeking to know his name. Kit was telling her when her husband interrupted.

'Where did you find that, young man?' Once again he was sharp, and the wrinkles in his forehead deepened. 'What made you bring it here?'

The old man's angry glare turned Kit into an unwelcome stranger. Now he was facing the Tom Townsend he feared. 'I'm sorry,' he muttered and turned away, beginning to rewrap the blade. Even the shuffle of his feet sounded guilty.

'Mister Kit!' It was the old lady. 'I would really like to know what brought you here.' She was indignant, but Kit was not her target for she turned to her husband. 'I really don't know what's got into you, Tom.'

Kit looked at them. Both were grim-faced, even if for different reasons, and he guessed his own expression was no better. But then, quite unexpectedly, the old man looked sideways at his wife and she glanced haughtily back at him, their eyes met and their indignation somersaulted into laughter.

It took half a minute for Connie Townsend to hold up the blade and admit, 'But I still don't know what this thing is!'

Where was he to begin? Kit fumbled for a moment, then said, 'I found it in Dutchman's Cut . . .' but had to stop because the old man held up his hand and almost shouted, 'My skate ... the one I lost ... sixty years ago!'

And his wife joined in. 'Dutchman's Cut!' she cried. 'It can't be that, surely ... that's where you went through the ice.'

'Got a good soaking.' The pleasure at seeing the skate suddenly faded from her husband's face. 'Thought I was going to drown. I felt I was being pulled down by something underneath.'

His wife tried to reassure him. 'But all the time it was just the awful weight of your clothes. It took two of us to pull you out ... with a bit of help.'

'But in the end ...' Tom Townsend held up the blade '... all I lost was the blade of a single skate.'

They both turned to Kit and he told them of his own plunge into the black water with Joe and his struggle to bring the clump of weed to the bank. 'It clung to me,' he said. 'I just couldn't let go,' and he heard Connie Townsend draw in her breath.

'I very much hope you have been getting into serious trouble with your parents, young man,' she said. 'It was a dangerous thing to do.'

'Don't make it worse for the young feller, Connie.' Tom Townsend had screwed up his eyes and was smiling at Kit. 'He was no more looking for danger than I was, but it sometimes comes looking for you. I wasn't trying to test my footing under the bridge as you seem to think, I was just about to skate under the shadow of that bridge when a sheet of ice broke off and reared up in front of me like a great mouth opening and . . .'

'Was it a fish?' The words escaped as Kit again felt the heave of fear when he had glimpsed the huge shape under the bridge.

'Of course it wasn't!' Connie Townsend was indignant, but her husband was smiling.

'But at that first moment, Connie my dear, you also thought I was about to be swallowed up.'

'Well,' she said, 'it was getting dark and, just as you disappeared, the shadow under the bridge *did* seem to open up and you *did* go under.'

He nodded, not smiling now. 'And I sank right down to the mud at the bottom . . . that's when I lost my skate.'

'Oh, I can't bear to think of it!' Connie Townsend shuddered, but her husband smiled and changed the subject.

'Don't you think, Connie, that this young man deserves something for going to all this trouble?' he said.

Kit had not thought like this. A reward was going to spoil the story, and Connie Townsend saw what was on his mind. She turned to her husband. 'Stuff and nonsense, Tom Townsend, all he wants is to have lunch with us and tell us all about himself.'

But it was her husband who saw that the idea made Kit stiffen with embarrassment and he winked and said, 'Don't worry – the food's pretty good.'

And so it turned out. The old couple made it easy for him, and dusk came almost before Kit was aware of it. Tom Townsend had been silent for a while before he suddenly said, 'A single skate is of no use to anyone,' and he turned to Kit. 'Do you mind if I have this blade for a minute or two?'

'It's yours really.' Kit handed it to him and Tom left the room.

Now it was Connie Townsend's turn to fall silent and when Kit glanced at her he saw that she was breathlessly looking through the window at her husband in the garden. 'You've no idea how brave he is,' she murmured.

Her tension spread to Kit who could not bring himself to ask what she meant and both were holding their breath when Tom Townsend reached a shed beyond the lawns, slowly opened the door and entered the darkness. A moment later a light came on, and through the shed window they saw him among the shelves.

'He's done it!' Connie Townsend had her hands clasped and she was beaming as she turned to Kit. 'He has suffered the most terrible nightmares for years,' she said. 'Sometimes they seem to come in the daytime and when that happens he is afraid to leave the house for fear of what he may see. Like ghosts, he says. I ask him what they look like but he won't tell me ... but just occasionally, when I have held his hand, I have thought I have seen shapes ... something just standing and watching, never making the least sound, but watching ... always watching.'

She switched on the light in the room and stood in the window. 'Let him see us, Kit, so he knows we're here.'

They stood and watched him moving about in the shed – it was his workshop, she told Kit – but he did not once look away from whatever was holding his attention, and Connie Townsend eventually turned to Kit. 'I wonder what you're thinking about two silly old people who believe they see ghosts.' She smiled and held up a hand. 'Don't answer that, Kit. He really did believe he saw something awful under that bridge all those years ago, and he's never been able to get it out of his mind.'

The garden was darker now and the little square of light was so like a distant cinema screen that, for a moment, Kit wondered if there were other watchers in the garden. His eyes roamed the shadows and every bush seemed to be a figure stretching forward to see what was happening inside the workshop.

It became too real and suddenly he was speaking to block out the thought.

'Mr Townsend very nearly drowned,' he said loudly. 'When you have a big fright like that you can easily imagine you see things.'

At that moment the light in the workshop went out and Connie Townsend gripped Kit's hand. 'You shouldn't have to be watching all this,' she said as they heard the workshop door close and saw Tom Townsend making his way through the shadows. He seemed to be walking deliberately slowly and his wife said, 'What did I tell you, Kit – he's just proving to himself he's got nothing to worry about.'

Her husband came into the room. 'Here's something for you, Kit,' he said and held out a pair of ice skates. 'Fen runners – the very pair I was using when it happened.' The blade had been polished and fitted back into the wooden base where it belonged.

Kit tried to thank him, but the old man shook his head. 'Connie will tell you that I never throw anything away, but all I ever needed to make them as good as new was the blade . . . I think I was waiting for you to turn up.'

The darkness had deepened before Kit left and street lamps raised sparks of light into the bare branches of the trees the whole length of the avenue. The old couple stood at the door to see him safely to the gate and he was turning to wave them goodbye when his arm brushed against something in the gloom. He jerked back and saw a figure standing silently on the pavement, gazing at him. The shock had made him angry and he was about to speak when a second surprise silenced him. The figure was a girl.

'Sorry,' he said and would have added more except that history seemed to be repeating itself and he recognised her. She was the girl who had blundered into him in the shop doorway. And once again she was not alone and he had to shuffle his bike out of the gateway to let them both through.

She closed the gate and he was about to ride away when, suddenly, she leant forward and said something. It was no more than a murmur and he could not make out her words. He stopped and turned towards her.

'Tomorrow.' She had raised her voice slightly, but he still had to struggle to hear what she said. 'I'll be at the old horse trough tomorrow – two o'clock.' She drew back and was already a pace away from the gate when she turned her head and said over her shoulder, 'Tell no one!'

The last he saw of her was as she entered the house with the old couple.

FIVE

THE HIDING PLACE

The old horse trough had a high stone back that made it look like a neglected sofa standing in the corner of the market place. Jenny stood in its shadow and gazed along the rows of bright stalls towards the glittering pyramid of the Christmas tree at the far end of the square and wondered if the boy she had met in the gateway would turn up. Why should he? She did not know him. It was only the way he had hesitated when speaking to her, as if he thought she had someone with her, that had made her act so impulsively. Did he even know of the horse trough? Was he aware it was a meeting place?

She tilted her head back and looked at the sky where the stars were already visible and she felt the comfort of the grey fur collar of her short jacket. What if he thought this was a date? Why hadn't she worn something plain, even dowdy? She had taken a step towards the shadows when a voice halted her.

'I'm a bit late,' he said. 'I couldn't see you at first.'

He didn't ask why she wanted to see him. That meant he thought this *was* a date. She was gazing at him, unable to think how to reply, when his eyes left her face and looked beyond her. He disliked her, she thought.

What he was thinking was that her face, nestling in the soft fur, was a great deal prettier than the girl he had seen in the shadows of the gateway. He was afraid she could easily read his thoughts so he pretended that his attention had been caught by something behind her.

'What ...?' she began, and looked over her shoulder. There were people moving in and out of the pools of light around the stalls but, at no more than four paces away from her, the heaped apples of a fruit stall were made hazy by a misty column of shadow.

He saw the change in her expression as she turned

back to him. Her dark eyes were wide, and she was no longer shy.

'So you see it, too!' She was leaning forward, keeping her voice low. 'There's something standing behind me, watching.'

Kit saw nothing very clearly.

'Like yesterday afternoon,' she insisted, 'in my grandfather's gateway.'

His eyes no longer searched the background. 'Your grandfather?'

She did not understand why he was so surprised. She looked back over her shoulder. The light from the stall was too bright and customers were too close. 'It's gone now,' she said, 'but you did see it yesterday ... someone watching me in the gateway?'

'I may have seen something,' he muttered. 'I'm not sure.' His mind was still placing her as a member of the Townsend family.

'After you left yesterday they told me all about you,' she said, and then neither could think of anything more to say until they had left the bustle of the market and were walking along a quieter street. She halted and, without looking directly at him, said, 'Something watches me. I call it the Watcher, but no one else has ever seen it ... no one, until you came along.' Then, embarrassed, she hurried on for a few steps before he caught up.

'Is it there now?' he asked.

She looked carefully around her and then said softly as though she was afraid of being overheard, 'In front of that shop over there . . . in front of the window.'

There could have been something hazy there, but he wasn't sure. There were people walking by.

'This is a bad place.' She was suddenly so disappointed he felt sorry for her.

'What does it look like?' he asked. 'Is it a man?'

'It was in the shop doorway when you saw it for the first time – and you saw it in the gateway yesterday.' She had raised her voice. 'Of course it's like a man! But tall . . . very tall!'

He desperately wanted to agree with her. 'Well, there *were* shadows,' he said. 'Each time I did *see* something.'

The doubt in his voice made her impatient. She was no longer shy. She took him by the hand and said, 'There's one place I know that is worse than all the others,' and she led him to where the street ended facing the railings of a public garden. They turned into a backwater that led into a little square that was quite deserted. One side was taken up with a flight of steps leading to the doorway of the town's museum.

She was embarrassed to find that she was still holding his hand and she released his fingers. 'Sorry,' she murmured, but he had already moved ahead to open the door and they stepped into utter silence. There was not even an attendant at the desk but as the door closed behind them a man, the curator, peered at them from the doorway of an office, nodded and retreated.

Their careful footsteps seemed to make less sound than the rustle of their clothing as they drifted through an archway into the heart of the museum. Lamps hanging on long cords like lonely spiders put a cold gleam on the glass of the cabinets and as they moved into another gallery even further from the foyer Jenny paused. She did not want her voice to be heard in so great an area of still air, and Kit had to bend his head so that he was looking at the floor as she whispered, 'There's a place just ahead of us where I was looking at some . . .'

She broke off. Her eyes were wide, darker than even the darkest shadows in the corners of the large room, but although she was looking at him she saw nothing. She was listening, and from the next gallery there came the sound of a shuffling footstep. 'There's someone else,' she whispered, and they waited until the footsteps slowly retreated before they edged forward. The gallery was empty, but Kit was aware that every step they took into this labyrinth of rooms led them further and further away from the lights and the holly and mistletoe of the market stalls and into the darker side of winter.

They had reached the centre of the museum where the ceiling reached even higher and a gallery ran around all four walls and looked down on them.

Moving quicker now, Jenny went to a display table with a glass top and was about to lean over it when she drew back with a look of disgust. The glass had a smear as if someone with a muddy finger had been pointing out something in the display beneath. Kit wiped it away with his sleeve and they both bent over the glass.

'Things from the fens,' she said. She was nervous and her voice was little more than a whisper. 'One of them is very important.'

There was a sickle that fenmen of long ago had used for cutting reeds, a whetstone to sharpen it, a five-pronged eel spear, fragments of bone, and clay models of animals that ancient tribes had offered to their gods. There was also a small disc that seemed to be made of oyster shell. It had all the lustre of mother-of-pearl and she seemed particularly interested in it, but said nothing.

What was the point of looking at all this? Why was he even here? Kit raised his head to ask the question just as she pulled back her sleeve to show that she wore a charm bracelet which she slipped from her

wrist and held in front of him. She was smiling as
though there was something about it he should notice.

'What's so special?' he asked.

'This.' She pointed to one of the charms, and he
saw it was a mother-of-pearl disc identical to the one
in the exhibition case. 'I call it my pearl shell,' she
said. 'It's what makes the Watcher appear.'

She had an uncertain smile, hoping he would
believe her, but he could not hold her gaze and looked
away. As he did so he heard her sharp little gasp of
disappointment at his reaction but he said nothing.

'I'm sure the Watcher is always there,' she insisted,
'but it only becomes really clear when I'm touching
the pearl shell. My bracelet is the hiding place for it.'

He wanted to know why she should hide it.

'Because my mother and father don't like it. They
believe I'm seeing things that aren't there ... they
think I'm making it all up and they worry about me.'

'But I think I see the Watcher ... at times.'

'You're the only one.'

At that Kit's doubts returned. A few misty shadows
did not truly make a Watcher. He turned his head,
looking around. 'I see nothing now.'

Suddenly Jenny was also peering into the shadows
of the long room. It was empty. There was no sign of
any Watcher, and Kit had reached for the bracelet to
see if touching the pearl shell made any difference

when it slipped from his fingers and fell with a clatter to the floor. The noise marked the end of everything. No strange shadow had appeared. There was no Watcher, and there never had been.

Kit turned to Jenny. Even she had seen nothing. 'So,' he said, 'we are quite safe after all.' He tilted his head back as he took a deep breath of relief, and he was still stretching when she saw his muscles lock and he remained gazing upwards. She tilted her own head, and she too stiffened.

Poised above them and leaning out from the gallery, its elbows as pointed as the wings of a bat, the misty figure of a man was gazing down at them.

Nothing moved in the silent hall, but Jenny's whisper reached him. 'You see it too . . .'

It was at that moment they heard steps from the foyer and the curator came bustling into the hall. He was frowning. 'I heard a noise,' he said. 'What was it?'

'I dropped my bracelet.' Jenny put it into her pocket.

'But did you see him?' The curator was angry, and Jenny spoke quickly to prevent Kit giving anything away. 'We've seen nothing,' she said. 'I think we're the only people here. The place is empty.'

'Well he was here a little while ago, before you came.' The curator was indignant. 'He's an old tramp who's taken it into his head to come in here out of the cold and he leaves his messy fingerprints all over the glass. I was sure I heard him shuffling about.'

They had seen his mark but there was no sign of the tramp, and the door of the museum had shut behind them and they were walking down the steps into the square when Jenny said, 'But you do see the Watcher.'

'It must have been the tramp.'

'No.' She was almost laughing. 'You saw the Watcher, as I knew you would. We are the same, we two ... and I know someone who will believe us!'

SIX

THE PEARL SHELL

Kit guessed where she was taking him, and he was glad of the snow that sprinkled their heads and shoulders as they crossed town. It was a disguise, a kind of protection as they stood before the black front door and Jenny tugged the bellpull. He was half-hidden behind her when Connie Townsend answered the door.

'Jenny!' Her grandmother was surprised. 'And you've brought a schoolfriend with you – how charming!'

It was as embarrassing as Kit had imagined, and it got worse.

'Good gracious, it's that boy!' Connie Townsend exclaimed, and she called over her shoulder, 'Tom! Jenny's brought her boyfriend to see us – and you'll never guess who it is.'

Indoors, food was produced, and hot drinks, and Kit felt the snowflakes dissolve on the back of his neck but somehow could not lift his hand to brush them away. It was Tom Townsend who noticed his discomfort and grinned. 'Serves you right,' he said. 'None of this would have happened if you'd never brought me my old skate.'

'And you, Tom,' his wife broke in, 'would never be as happy as you are this minute getting ready to bring the Cake House Café back to life.'

'Should never have closed it down,' he said.

'Be quiet, Tom. Jenny wants to ask you a question.'

'Grandad,' said Jenny slowly. Her voice was very small. 'You know I sometimes see things that no one else can see.'

The room became very quiet except that her grandmother drew in her breath sharply and, when no one else spoke, said gently, 'Please don't say it's still happening to you, Jenny. You know there's nothing awful there, my dear.'

Jenny was pale and her voice had become very small. 'I think Grandad said once that something like that had happened to him a long time ago.'

'Oh, that man!' Connie shook her head. 'He's always had far too much imagination – haven't you, Tom?'

Her husband did not deny it. His long, serious face showed a twinkle of amusement as he answered, 'When it first happened I'd just made a big fool of myself by plunging through the ice, Connie, and it was the shock that brought it on. For a while I thought I was seeing things.' He turned to his granddaughter. 'Just like you, Jenny.'

Connie was impatient. 'The pair of you have far too much imagination!' She turned to Kit. 'Just you tell that girl you won't stand any nonsense from her.'

Kit reddened and murmured something while Jenny turned her back, as if that would help take their eyes away from him, and spoke to her grandfather, 'Tell us what you found out after you fell through the ice, Grandad – all about the Worm.'

'Oh, not that again!' Connie turned to Kit. 'I expect you've heard about the Worm of Longlode Fen.'

Kit nodded, '. . . and I know it wasn't even a worm.'

Tom Townsend confessed, 'But there does seem to have been some big, scaly creature that lived in the waterways when the fens were wild. The Longlode Worm became a dragon that could swallow a whole ox at one go. Many people said they had seen it.'

Kit knew a little more. 'And wasn't there a tribe that

49

killed it because their chieftain had a magic sword?'

Tom Townsend nodded. 'And there are people out in the fens, or used to be when I was younger, who still say something went wrong and the Worm survived.' He smiled. 'There may still be some of them about.'

Jenny interrupted. 'And you told me all about that when I was little and we were walking along a riverbank ... I was terrified and thought the Worm was right there, in the water, at that very moment.'

He was laughing. 'But it was a good story ...'

'And you made it worse,' said Jenny. 'You picked something out of the mud and told me it was a dragon scale.'

'Just the sort of ridiculous thing he would do,' Connie broke in. 'Terrifying a little girl like that!'

'It was nothing,' said Tom. 'Just a bit of pearly shell from a freshwater mussel – something like that.'

'But I believed it.' Jenny spoke very quietly. 'It cut my finger.'

Her grandmother reached out and held her hand. 'He should have known better,' she said, 'because he's just like you at heart. Things affect him in very much the same way.' She turned to her husband, 'Don't they, Tom? The pair of you always manage to make things worse than they are.'

Kit suddenly felt he was an outsider who knew too

much. At any moment Jenny would be talking about the Watcher and he wanted to reject it. There were too many dangers.

It was Connie Townsend who saved him. She turned to him and said, 'You see the sort of scrapes they used to get into, Kit – no wonder poor Jenny has had some trouble about feeling haunted, haven't you?'

So her grandparents did know something about Jenny and the Watcher, but before Jenny could say anything Tom Townsend added, 'Well, I have to admit that going through the ice made me feel very spooky for a time.'

'And you still do,' his wife added.

'But I got over it. And you will soon put it all behind you, won't you, Jenny?'

There was silence for a moment, and Kit was sure that Jenny was about to tell everyone that he, too, was able to see the Watcher, when her grandmother turned to him and changed the subject.

'They tell me,' she said, 'that a lot of people are skating on the canal, and I wondered if you had been able to try out your fen runners.'

Kit was admitting he had not yet had a chance to test them when Tom Townsend got out of his chair and went out into the snow.

'Just look at that silly man,' said his wife, 'out there without a coat at his age.'

But when he came back he was carrying a pair of skate boots. 'They were yours when you were a bit younger, Connie,' he said.

'I was only a girl when I last wore them.' She was laughing. 'I shall never use them again.'

'I remember sharpening the blades for you years ago and I've just given them a bit of a shine. I was wondering if they would fit Jenny.'

'Of course they would!' Connie was delighted, and in the fuss of Jenny trying them on and lacing them up, she made sure that Jenny's feelings of being haunted were not mentioned again.

SEVEN

SNOWSTORM

As they came out of the house so much snow was drifting on the breeze that Connie Townsend had closed the front door even before they reached the garden gate. Kit hardly noticed.

'You didn't tell them that I could see your Watcher,' he said.

'It's not *mine* – I don't want it!' There were snow-flakes on Jenny's black hair and he hoped she would not spoil the way she looked by pulling up her hood. But she did.

Dark clouds hung so heavily over the avenue that

the trees seemed to be lit only by the whiteness of the snow.

'Can you see it now?' He was impatient with her, as if she was refusing to let him into a secret that belonged only to her family.

'No.' She had the bracelet in her pocket.

'Well why don't you let me handle the dragon scale to see if it really does work for me?'

She stopped walking and turned towards him. 'I just wanted you to hear from my grandfather how I came to get it.'

She seemed to be making a mystery even of that. 'Well?'

She looked around her. The avenue was almost deserted but an occasional person was hurrying by, head bent against the snow.

'Let's go somewhere we'll not be interrupted,' and she tugged at his hand.

He was not familiar with this part of town and he had no idea where she was taking him along quiet roads blurred by snow, but they went through a barrier of trees into what he sensed must be a wide open space. The breeze had quickened and picked up so much snow that he could see no more than a few yards ahead.

'This is as good a place as any,' she said, and they stood with their backs to the wind as she fumbled with her gloves and took off her bracelet. He watched as she searched through the dangling charms to find the pale disc that, even in the dimness of the snow-storm, had the faint rainbow glimmer of mother-of-pearl.

'I've told everyone I threw it away,' she said. 'They made me promise. You're the only one who knows I hide it in my bracelet.'

They were walled in by snow as she separated the dragon scale from the other charms. 'No one else knows about it.'

He examined the disc as it lay on her palm. It was exactly like the one in the museum.

'I know it's only a piece of shell from something living out in the fens,' she said, 'but when people find one they call it a dragon scale because it looks as if it comes from something large, like a dragon.'

'The Worm of Longlode,' he murmured. But that was no more than a story from the distant past when dragons were said to roam the land. Pieces of oyster shell had helped to build up the story over the centuries. Now, as they stood face to face, thoughts flew from one to the other. Jenny still had the dragon scale in her palm so that even now Kit should also be able to see the Watcher.

They lifted their heads. A white wall, as soft as sea foam, hemmed them in. The boundaries of the clearing were lost and they were totally alone. Even their footprints had already been smoothed away. As Kit gazed into the blankness his mind slid to Dutchman's Cut and the clump of weed he had dredged from the depths. 'A bit of shell cut my finger then,' he said aloud, 'but no one called it a dragon scale.'

Jenny did not seem to have heard him. She was peering into the blizzard. At some distance from them a swirl of snow seemed to hang greyly in the air and slowly thickened until it became a shape coming towards them. Kit had the urge to back away and find a road where he could be with people and it was only because Jenny held her ground that he stood firm. She had told him that the Watcher shadowed her but never came close.

He turned towards her. She was gazing at the figure, but this time it was already closer than ever before and still advancing. They were both shuffling back, hampered by the deep snow, when Kit put his hand on Jenny's arm. The figure was not the tall shadow with the large, drooping head that he had seen in the museum. It was smaller, no taller than Kit himself, and was already making tracks to avoid them when Kit called out to it. The figure was Joe ploughing his way through the blizzard.

Joe was slow to recognise the girl with Kit, but when he did so his eyes became as cold as the wind.

She was the crazy girl who belonged to the family who had sacked his uncle.

Kit tried to explain why they were together. 'Jenny knows about the ice skate we found in Dutchman's Cut,' he said.

'What ice skate?' Joe was deliberately ignorant.

Kit tried again. 'Jenny knows quite a lot about things found out in the fens . . . at least her grandfather does.' To mention her grandfather to Joe was a mistake. Desperately Kit added, 'We've been trying to find out about things lost in the water . . . have you ever heard of dragon scales?'

Kit saw Jenny stiffen. It was a stupid thing to ask, but Joe's reply was brusque. 'No. I've never heard of anything like that.' He looked briefly at Jenny, but ignored Kit. 'I've got to go,' and he trudged past them and was soon lost in the blizzard.

Jenny was gazing down at her hands and for a moment Kit was sure she had been hurt by Joe's aloofness, but when she looked up it was not because her feelings had been hurt. There was panic in her face.

'It's gone!' she cried. 'I've lost my dragon scale!'

They searched where she was standing, stroking away layers of snow, but the rainbow shimmer of the little disk did not appear, and the wider they searched the more panic-stricken Jenny became.

'The Watcher may be here right now,' she cried, 'but we shall never know, and no one will ever believe me. You were the only one!' She stood gazing into the blizzard as if she was willing the Watcher to appear, but what shadows there were dissolved into swirls of snow.

Kit's head was bowed. He was thinking back. 'I know there was a disc just like it when I found the skate . . . it cut my finger . . . I remember it.'

Jenny, clutching at his hand, said, 'What happened to it?'

He forced himself to look into her eyes.

'I threw it away,' he said.

EIGHT

THE NIGHT VISITOR

Kit helped his father bring down the boxes of decorations from the loft. It was the sign that Christmas had begun, but this time the glitter and sparkle were too fragile to hold his mind from the windswept bleakness of the park. Any chance of solving the mystery of the dragon scales had been blown away in the blizzard. Jenny Townsend may have been afraid of the Watcher but now that she no longer had the means of seeing it there seemed to be no reason for her to call on Kit. He had not seen her for two days.

'Hook that end up over the bookcase,' said his mother as she handed him a paper streamer which he allowed to concertina to the floor. 'What's got into you, Kit? You look half asleep!'

'It's his girlfriend,' said his father.

'What girlfriend?' His mother was suspicious.

'There *is* no girlfriend.' Kit did not blush. There was no need. He had walked with Jenny to her door, but all contact between them had been lost in the snow of the park. There was no Watcher.

'Well I know who she *was*,' said his father. He had brought the tree in from outside and was putting it in the corner it always occupied. 'I saw the two of them in the market place just the other day.'

Kit winced. His father's work took him everywhere. Why had he not noticed him?

'And I know *who* she is.' His father was talking into the corner, not looking at him. 'It's the Townsend girl ... quite pretty if you like them with large dark eyes.'

Kit remained silent. It was all over. Why should he bother to deny it? But his mother had not yet heard enough.

'I don't know any Townsends,' she said.

'Oh yes you do ... they have the cake shop in Market Street.'

'But that's been closed for years.'

'What do you know about it, Kit?' His father,

having settled the tree, turned to the room. 'There seemed to be lot of people working on it when I went by.'

'How would I know?' said Kit. 'It's nothing to do with me.'

'Don't worry.' His father was grinning. 'We've all been jilted at least once in our lives.'

'Speak for yourself,' said Kit's mother.

They were laughing, but Kit had gone to his room. Outside his window snow decorated trees and hedges, but all the mysteries had disappeared and soon he was asleep.

It could not have been a sound that woke him. The house was in the grip of winter and utterly silent, and he sensed it was the dead of night. He lay in darkness with the window only visible because of the faint glimmer of the snow outside, yet something had stirred deep in his mind to make him open his eyes.

He slid from under his duvet like a bear pushing out of a snowdrift and stepped silently to the window. His eyes were watchful but his mind was with the moment when the dragon scale was snatched away in the blizzard.

He gazed into the silent night. Jenny's finger had been cut by the dragon scale when she had first picked it up. The same had happened to him but then, carelessly, not knowing what he was doing, he had thrown his own dragon scale away. He felt hollowed out by his own stupidity.

The next instant he was pulling on his clothes. He could never have been so insensitive as to throw out a thin circle of shell that glinted with rainbow colours. At the very worst he would have laid it aside and then forgotten it. That would have been when he was cleaning rust from the blade of the skate from Dutchman's Cut. The bench in the garden shed. That's where it was.

He went silently down to the kitchen. There was a flashlight in a drawer but the battery was dead. He would search the bench with his fingertips.

His boots creaked in the snow as he crossed the yard to the shed. The key turned easily in the lock, the door opened silently and he stepped inside into the smell of oily rags and old potato sacks. And something else. There was a mustiness, as if some animal had made its den in the shadows and he felt a spasm of fear as the door clicked shut behind him. He was turning towards it when a voice said, 'It ain't worth your while to run.'

Nothing prevented him lunging for the handle but the door, which had swung open so easily, had jammed.

'It ain't no use tryin',' said the voice, but Kit was

still heaving at the handle as he turned to look over his shoulder.

The window could have been the pale page of a book for all the light it gave, but the voice had jolted his memory and now he could make out a bulky figure by the bench.

'I been waitin' for you,' said Old Cottle.

Kit made an effort to swallow his panic but his voice trembled as he said, 'I didn't know you slept in here.'

'It don't matters much where I sleep.'

'No,' Kit agreed, 'I don't suppose it does.' Old Cottle's rags were thicker than any sleeping bag, and rain would never penetrate far. But he was doing no harm in the shed, so he could be left where he was. 'I think I've got to go back to bed,' Kit said weakly.

He was ignored. 'You come here lookin' for somethin',' said the old man.

'It doesn't matter.' Kit knew he was being feeble. 'I'll try again in daylight.'

In reply, Old Cottle shuffled until he was within what little light came from the window and he raised a hand so Kit could see he held something that glinted faintly and said, 'I seen you pick this out o' the mud.'

It was the size and shape of the dragon scale. It must have been among the rags on the bench. Kit said nothing.

'There's another one of these,' said the old man. 'It belongs to a young maid.'

'Not any more.' Kit's courage was returning and he did not fear to contradict. 'She lost her dragon scale in the snow.'

There was no sound, but the glint of the scale vanished as Old Cottle's fingers closed over it. The night was still, and the silence deepened within the shed until his voice rumbled once more. 'You got to take it to her so she'll know when dangers come.'

Kit could just make out that he seemed to wrap the dragon scale in a scrap of rag torn from his sleeve before handing it over. 'No one must touch it but that young maid,' he said. 'She is the one at gravest risk. Do not even look at it before you give it to her. And at this time tomorrow night you got to bring her to where you first set eyes on me.'

'You mean the bridge on Dutchman's Cut?' Kit did not believe what he had heard.

'That's where you saw me, ain't it?'

'But how can we get there ... in all this snow ... and there's no proper road?'

'The dykes is all froze, and you've got these.' As he spoke the old man reached to the hook where Kit's fen runners hung and let them clatter to the bench. 'You got these, and she have her skates ... there's a ice road all the way.'

Kit's mind was numb, but before he could utter a word the old man was speaking again. 'Them blades you have got – and her skates also – have felt the kiss of the stone and they are keen. They will bring you to me.'

'What stone?'

But the old man had stepped past him and had already reached the door. 'Midnight,' he said, 'when all will be asleep. You have no choice.'

The snow had come again and a breeze made it press white fingers against the window pane. Without another word the old man opened the door and stepped outside. The last Kit saw of him was his hunched figure, already coated with snow, shuffling along the lane and into the darkness.

NINE

THE CAKE SHOP CAFÉ

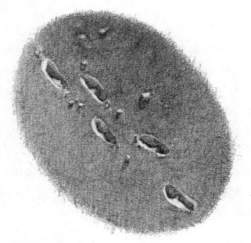

In the morning Kit looked for evidence of what had happened. Overnight snow had smoothed away all footprints, and it was not until he put his hand in his pocket and found a small wad of rags that the meeting with Old Cottle seemed to become less of a dream. He remembered the old man's words and he dared not unwrap the rags.

He was silent at breakfast but the thought of night skating made him smile and when his father asked what was amusing him he said, 'I was just wondering if I could skate out as far as Dutchman's Cut.'

'On those old fen runners? Even Babs Horn could hardly do half a mile on them.'

'I could try.'

'You will do no such thing!' his mother butted in. 'The water's deep out there, and you'll drown.'

'But the ice must be thick by now.'

'Not as thick as you are if you try it,' said his father.

'Thanks, Dad.'

'Don't mention it, my boy, and pass the toast.'

After that Kit felt light-headed about what had seemed to have happened in the night, and even if he really had spoken to Old Cottle in the shed there was not the slightest possibility of taking Jenny to see him so far out in the fens ... and in the middle of the night. All he could do was tell her what seemed to have happened.

And a new problem faced him when he got off the bus in town. He had never called at her house in the Crescent and he could not think what he would say if one of her parents should answer the door, so he wandered aimlessly through the streets to delay the moment and half-hoping to see Jenny before he got there.

Winter had fastened its grip on the town. Frozen snow was piled in the gutters but every shop window was bright and the pavements were thronged. He began to feel very much part of it when one or two older people smiled at the sight of the fen runners slung around his neck, and he had come to the end of Market Street before he realised that something had changed. He looked back. The gleaming shopfronts made a bright wall along both sides of the street. There were no gaps ... yet he felt there was something missing. He let his glance wander back along the street, and then he saw it. Where there should have been a black iron grille with a blank window behind it there was nothing but glitter. He walked towards it and saw that, under the glare of bare bulbs, carpenters were putting up new shelves and painters were at work on the stairs leading to the café above.

'And you are to blame,' said a man's voice behind him. 'All this expense is because of you.'

His mind jerked back to the time, only a few weeks ago, when he had poked at the grimy window through a black grille. He must have damaged something, and now he was being blamed. He spun around ... and was face to face with Jenny's grandfather.

Tom Townsend was grimy but he was grinning. 'You are responsible for all this,' he said. 'You and my granddaughter.'

Kit was about to apologise but Tom Townsend went on, 'You two set Connie and I thinking about old times here – especially in winter when we always had a big party upstairs in the café ... and suddenly we realised how much we missed the old place, so here we are with a week to go and no time to linger talking to the likes of you, my boy.' He paused. 'You'll find Jenny upstairs.'

Even more embarrassment awaited Kit when he had climbed the stairs. It was a large room with one very tall window looking down onto Market Street and it was as though he was standing on an open stage when he saw Jenny bringing large cardboard boxes from a side room. She blushed to see him there, but before either of them had said a word a man came into the room calling her by name and she was introducing Kit to her father.

'So you're the one I've been hearing about,' he said.

'Not from me,' said Jenny, but then her shyness deepened and she looked at the floor.

'Well, maybe not her,' said the man, who looked remarkably like her grandfather when he grinned. 'But you're the one who's made me change my job because I'm coming back to work here as I did in the old days. What's your name again? – I didn't properly hear my daughter's mumble.'

'Kit.'

'Well, Kit, are those the famous skates dangling around your neck?'

'I was going to ask Jenny to come skating on the

canal.' There was some chance that parts of the ice had been swept clear of snow.

'She's never skated in her life.' Her father was laughing. 'So I hope you return her in one piece – she's got work to do here.'

Once out in the street Jenny let her anger show. 'You needn't think you're going to return me anywhere,' she said. 'And, anyway, what sort of skater are *you*?'

He did not want to say, and he had still not told her about the visit from Old Cottle in the middle of the night. He was beginning to doubt that it had taken place.

They said little as they walked to the Crescent, and Jenny let herself in to an empty house. 'My mother must be out buying things for that old cafe,' she said. 'No one thinks of anything else.'

Kit was relieved at not having to meet another member of her family, but Jenny was adding another problem. 'My father's right,' she said, 'the only time I ever tried to skate I couldn't do it.' She had opened a cupboard under the stairs and was reaching into the darkness for her skates. 'I know I put them here,' she said.

'I don't think it matters,' he said.

'What do you mean?' She had backed out of the cupboard and was holding her skate boots in triumph. 'I want to try them out anyway.'

He did not seem to have heard her. 'I met someone last night,' he began, but she did not want to listen.

'Skating!' She was laughing. 'All I can do is fall over!'

Kit was laughing with her as they walked along the canal bank trying to find a deserted place where they could make their first attempt. It was impossible; the ice was crowded.

In some ways it was more embarrassing for Kit. He had skated before this, but not for a long time and never with any skill. Now, when he had strapped on his ancient fen runners and he and Jenny were hobbling down the bank, they were both aware of spectators.

Kit was first to step on to the ice but kept himself upright only by clinging to Jenny, who was still on the bank. Then he splayed out his blades and held steady while Jenny put one foot on the ice and almost twisted her ankle as her taller skates threw her off balance. She prevented herself doing the splits only by jamming her feet against Kit's.

They rocked, almost falling, waiting for their feet to slide from under them and send them thudding to the ice in a heap. But they held together, swaying, beginning to totter and well aware that they were on a stage with an audience all around them.

How it happened they could never afterwards be

sure except that they were suddenly upright and as steady as if they were on firm ground. Jenny was the first to free herself, stand motionless and sense the rock-hard ice through the sharp edges of her blades. When she let herself move it was as if a pendulum had been released and she was swinging in a great arc away from Kit. She guessed that she was watched from the banks and even by other skaters on the ice, but she did not focus on anyone. She could fly, but knew that if she thought about it she would fall.

Then Kit was alongside her and they curved and cut their way through other skaters and past the houses until they reached the edge of town and the ice was clear. They circled to a standstill and gazed at each other, startled and half afraid of what was happening.

They could hear the shouts and laughter of other skaters in the distance, but here, where the low winter sun sparkled on banks of untouched snow, there was silence.

Kit looked down at the ice and slid one of his fen runners to and fro. 'Are you tired?' he asked.

'No,' said Jenny. 'I could go on for hours.'

Neither had worn skates for years and had been clumsy even at their best, but now the gentlest thrust caused them to glide as if they touched nothing underfoot. They were already in a strange world in which Kit knew that Jenny was to be asked to take great risks. It was then that Kit told her, 'I met someone who told me the blades of my skates had touched *the stone*.'

'What stone did they mean?'

Kit was unable to tell her. 'If my skates have touched some stone or other,' he said, 'yours must have done the same.'

Her skate boots made her as tall as Kit on his flat fen runners and they gazed directly at each other as if they needed to be told that what had just happened was true. They smiled only slightly, afraid to break the spell.

It was Jenny who had the courage to speak.

'Old Cottle,' she said. Kit seemed to have forgotten he had already told her about the tramp he had met last summer. Now she had guessed Kit had seen him again.

'He was there when I went out of the house to look for the dragon scale I lost,' he told her.

'Did you find it?'

He did not seem to have heard her question; there was something more pressing on his mind. 'He knows about you,' Kit said.

'What does he know?' She was suspicious. 'Is it something you told him?'

Kit shook his head. 'He knows many things – and he wants to see you.'

'Why me? I've got nothing to do with him – I've never even seen him!' She was panicking and thrust herself away and began to glide towards the safety of the town.

He caught up with her and, without thinking how it was done, reached in front of her and held the hand furthest away from him. Next moment their other hands met and they were leaning forward together, arms crossed in front of them, and skating in long sweeps left and right back towards the crowd, and so convincing that other skaters gave them space and watched them go by.

'Tonight,' said Kit as they took off their skates and climbed the bank. 'He wants to see you tonight.'

She did not reply. Instead she said, 'I've got work to do,' and he walked with her back to the café.

She was silent while Kit was helping her remove the last bags of rubbish from the restaurant upstairs, and they had walked into the kitchen adjoining the large room when she said suddenly, 'I can't do it . . . I won't go out in the middle of the night to see a mad old tattered man!'

'He says he's got to see you . . . it's got to be you.'

'But why me?'

Kit did not know. All he could remember was the old man saying: 'I got to see the maid. She's the only one that can help.'

He tried again. 'There's the skates,' he said. 'We didn't know we could skate until we tried them – and suddenly we were better than anyone else.'

She walked through to the restaurant where some of the tables and chairs were already in place and stood by the large window looking out into the street. It was snowing again. She had seen no Watcher since she had lost her dragon scale in the blizzard. Her imagination had been too strong. Why should she bring it all back by skating out into the fens in the middle of the night?

It was all in the past. She looked at Kit to tell him so.

He had taken something from his pocket and was unwrapping it. He folded back scraps of rag and held it out for her to see.

'I found it last night,' he said. 'It must have been in the garden shed all the time.'

His dragon scale lay there. She was afraid and would not touch it so it was Kit who ignored Old Cottle's order and picked it out of its ragged nest ... but it was Jenny who saw the tall, thin shape of the Watcher in the shadows at the back of the room. She knew then that she had to obey the old ragged man she had never seen.

TEN

BLACK ICE

Jenny came silently from her room at the top of the
house and looked down the well of the stairs. It was
a dark pit in which a slight shift in the air was mag-
nified into the breathing of some night wanderer
climbing towards her ... and then the skates hanging
around her neck swung together and the click of
steel blades was loud enough to penetrate her parents'
room. She held her breath, but now the only sound
was the rustle of her scarf as she muffled the blades.

She went down into the darkness but before she
reached the hall her mind was suddenly clouded with

doubts. Everything that had happened had begun with herself. Kit would not have been dragged into this if they had never met. She would tell him so.

Kit had not kept his promise. He was not at the edge of town waiting for her as she expected. The risk of letting her cross the town alone at night had weighed on his mind, so now he was huddled on a seat in the little public garden that faced the houses of the Crescent and he was shivering. It was madness to believe they could skate into the darkness to meet an old man far out in the fens.

On the stairs Jenny was breathing easier. All of this had come about because her own imagination was in turmoil. There would be no wild journey into the black fens tonight.

Kit saw the door of the house across the street swing back into darkness and he stood up. Jenny was there. He walked into the centre of the road to meet her.

Neither spoke. Even in this lack of light they could sense that they each believed they should not be here. Everything could be explained, and they would both see that the night held no mysteries.

Kit hesitated, then made up his mind to speak. She saw his lips part and, knowing that she would have to interrupt and disappoint him, she thrust her hand deep into her pocket and closed her fist over her gloves bunched together ... but what she held was not gloves . . . it was a wad of rags wrapped around an edge that bit into her finger.

Kit saw Jenny's mouth open as she looked beyond him, but no words came. He twisted until he saw the bushes at his back. Snow lay on bare branches but the black heart of the shadows was moving. The Watcher was stepping towards them out of the darkness.

They fled together out of the Crescent and towards the centre of the town. Twice they turned, but each time the grey shadow was stepping silently behind them even though Jenny was no longer touching the dragon scale. She wiped the blood from her finger but it was not until they were on the banks of the canal that the Watcher faded and vanished.

They leant against a fence to put on their skates and went crabwise down the bank to where the ice was littered with debris from games played in daylight. They were uncomfortable and their skates were clumsy, all magic gone. It was stupidity to be staggering through the night in a town that was fast asleep, and sickening disappointment made them cling together on the ice so that they would not fall. They took unsteady steps through the debris until they found clear ice and then they went slowly forward until, gradually, their confidence returned, the wind was biting their cheeks, and they were swinging past rows of silent houses. They swept under a bridge where a solitary walker stopped suddenly to gaze at two figures that sped beneath him and disappeared into the distance with so little sound that he believed he had seen ghosts.

The town fell away and the canal curved to join a frozen waterway that lay between flat fields. The sky seemed to lift and expand and the noise of their skates was so thin it did not disturb the silence.

They were side by side but Jenny was having difficulty keeping up. She glanced at Kit's dark silhouette and saw that he had one arm behind his back and was leaning forward with the other swinging free like a pendulum that added to the thrust of his legs. She had not heard the man on the bus talking to Kit of the fen skaters of long ago but soon she was leaning forward as he did and they cut through the icy air together.

His village was two rows of dark houses frowning down on them as they sped past with giant strides and out into the glimmer of the white plain where they skated on narrow channels scoured clean by the wind and did not stop until they came to the foot of a bank.

'We climb,' he said, and they clawed their way up through the brittle grass. At the top Jenny was panting and hardly upright when she realised she was perched on the edge of a wide channel. Its sullen water was frozen into a roadway that reached in a dead straight line far into the distance and as she drew in her breath she heard Kit say, 'Dutchman's Cut.'

The whole plain had been frozen to silence, but then, far out, a motorbike yipped into a new gear and held its thin top note until it died in the far distance. Somewhere out there, as silent as a sleeping dog, lay Cottle's Bridge.

The untouched snow bunched in front of them and spilled out on to the ice as they slid down the bank and staggered on to the ice where Kit, stamping his feet to shed compacted snow from his blades, pointed silently in the direction they must go. The immense silence seemed to forbid him to speak.

They gathered speed easily, tilting their heads forward to prevent the air biting the back of their throats, and each long stride pushed the snow banks faster and faster behind them but at each thrust Kit felt he was falling further and further into a trap. History was repeating itself. The ice under the bridge would be wet and rotten, and his skates were luring him into the same plunge that Jenny's grandfather had made all those years ago. He and Tom Townsend had each felt the grip of deep water and it was waiting for him again. He sensed it reaching for him and suddenly, in a panic, he leant back and with all his force dug his steel edges hard into the surface. There was a shower of ice that caught Jenny off guard and she was yards ahead before she pulled up and began to turn back to him.

She did not finish her circle. The stars above her went out and in the blackness all her movements echoed back to her. It was only when breath again shivered into her lungs that she saw she was in the shadow of a bridge. It was as if she was thrusting herself out of a cave as she turned to go back to him and she was still within the shadow when a voice directly above her made her lose her balance and fall. She was scrambling to stand upright when she heard a voice growling at her. Kit came to help her and as he stooped he murmured, 'It's him. He wants to see you on the bridge.'

But their skates would hinder them. They were safer on the ice. 'Why won't he come down?' she whispered.

The man could not have heard her, but what he said seemed to be a reply. 'You would do well to look down so you can see what is beneath your feet.'

They obeyed. There was no pool of melt water beneath the bridge. The ice was black and solid except for a scatter of crystals where their blades had cut into it.

'Look closer,' the voice demanded, and Kit crouched to brush the crystals aside.

Jenny also stooped. She had never known ice like

this. Even in this lack of light it was as pure as still water. She could even sense there was a great depth beneath it. Kit had swum there. She stiffened, trying not to shudder, and it was then, in the blackness below, that something moved. It was no more than a grainy hint, but a shape glided beneath them and sank away.

In a clumsy stutter of skates they fled to the bank and climbed to the frozen ruts of the track above but, once there, Jenny realised they were trapped. The skates prevented them running and the ice was a black pit of danger.

Kit's voice was tiny and useless under the stars but he gripped her hand and said anything to convince himself there was no danger. 'I've seen that before.' he muttered. 'It can't harm us.'

Jenny had lost all sense of belief that any of this was happening. The man on the bridge and themselves – three dark figures standing in a frozen wasteland – were no more than a picture in a book and she was dozing with it in her lap. She could will herself fully awake in an instant and be safe.

Then came the clatter of their skates on the planks of the bridge and they were standing two paces from the man Kit had called Old Cottle. He was made bulky with layers of rags as Kit had told her and his face was hardly visible under the peak of his cap. Then he spoke.

'It's a pity you ain't got nowhere to sit, young maid.'

Kit cleared his throat, suddenly wanting to laugh at this formality in the great wilderness of the night, but Jenny's voice was calm. 'I have come a long way,' she said.

'That you have . . . and so have I over the years.'

Jenny felt the bitter air on her cheeks. She knew she must be deathly pale, but all her fear had gone. Now the old man was taking off his cap and as he did so she was surprised to see that his hair was long and it swayed forward as he stooped as though he was bowing to her.

'There is no need,' she said. She did not know how the words came to her mouth, but she had sounded so grand, so queenly, that she added, 'I am just a girl.'

'It was a maid who saved my people when the Dragon's warriors came across the sea to rob us of our land,' said the old man. 'I offered my sword to the Maid of Fendyke Pool and she handed me the means to give it strength.'

Kit, seeing them talk as if they knew each other, felt the night slipping away from him. He had heard of deep pools in the fens where ancient tribes had made offerings to their gods '. . . but I've never heard of Fendyke Pool,' he said aloud. 'Where is it?'

He was still clad in rags, but Old Cottle had become a warrior. He pointed to the water directly below the bridge. 'It is in the deep silt beneath us. My sword was broken in battle and will never be seen again, but that which gave it power I returned to the pool and there it rested until the upheavals of recent times brought it to light.'

The night was sharp for all three, but Kit sensed that the keenest link was between Jenny and the old warrior. 'What was the gift that gave strength to your sword?' she said.

'A black whetstone no bigger than the palm of my hand. It gave an edge to my blade that nothing could withstand. When the stone had done its work I returned it to Fendyke Pool as I was pledged to do. The stone should rest there still, but it was stolen and it is free in the world again and the Dragon's whelps are seeking it.'

Kit's mind was racing. It was as if the old man's words were awakening ancient knowledge within himself, but there was still more that he did not know. Suddenly he found himself pointing along the length of Dutchman's Cut and demanding, 'What is it out there under the ice?'

For the first time Old Cottle took a step nearer them. 'Only those such as you who have been bitten by a dragon scale are aware of it,' he said, 'but the

Worm came from the sea with the invaders and grows great in the fresh fen waters. It can never return to the salt sea, and with its whelps it will ravage all the land unless the whetstone can be found to sharpen a weapon to slay it. *The whetstone must be found!'*

He had finished speaking and the silence grew so great that Kit could hardly find his voice and when it came it was little more than a whisper. 'What is the Watcher?' he asked.

'One of the Dragon's whelps. The others you have not yet seen but they bar me from the town where the whetstone lies.'

'How do they know it is there?'

For the first time what sounded like a chuckle rumbled in the old warrior's throat. 'Blades brought you to me tonight,' he said. 'Only blades that have felt the kiss of the whetstone could have made you glide through the night as smooth as a bird flies. The stone is somewhere near you and must be found.'

'And we must bring it to you?' Kit asked.

'No.' Old Cottle turned to Jenny. 'You must return it to Fendyke Pool.'

Jenny was troubled. The task was too great, too dangerous. 'Why me?' she asked quietly.

'A maid gave it, and a maid must return it to the pool where it belongs.' He broke off and raised his head as though he saw something in the distance and they looked in the same direction but saw nothing. When they turned back to him it was the same as when Kit had met him for the first time. Old Cottle was already at the far end of the bridge and moving away.

'What if we need you?' Kit called.

'You may find me in the Back of Beyond.' And he was gone.

ELEVEN

SHARP EDGES

It was a drab morning and Kit woke full of doubts. There had been no fresh snow so there should have been clear footprints if he had really gone out in the night and done all the things he seemed to remember, but when he looked out of his window the only hint of footprints was a few slight hollows in the snow that proved nothing. It was a grey morning with the suggestion of a thaw in the air, and when he tried to believe that Jenny had been with him, it all seemed even more unlikely.

Jenny had begun it all. She was a strange girl.

87

Everyone knew that, but her shy smile had made him want to believe everything she said. Perhaps he was the only one who had ever believed her. Perhaps by believing her he had made her fantasies even stronger. Perhaps he should not see her again.

It was all over. He went slowly down to breakfast not wanting to say a word to anyone about anything, and his father added more confusion. 'Here comes the ice champion of the century,' he said, and his mother looked closely at him and asked, 'Is it true?'

Kit was bewildered. Had he done something laughable, something that made him really foolish? They were both smiling, but his mother seemed uncomfortable, as if she wished it had never happened, whatever it was.

'You made a real exhibition of it – the pair of you.' His father's grin widened. 'You and the Townsend girl . . . taking to the ice like world champions. I didn't see you but I'm told that everyone was watching the two of you out there on the canal . . . cross hands like a pair of naturals . . . skating on and on and out of sight.'

So, if that was true in daylight, everything that had happened in the night could be more than a dream. 'And it was a long way to go at night,' he said. The words came out before he could hide them, and his mother was alarmed.

'At night?'

All he could do was to stammer that he had only just learned how to skate from Jenny. 'She's a very good skater,' he said. 'All I did was follow.'

'But at night?' she insisted.

'It will be night if I don't get into town soon for another lesson.'

It was a poor cover-up but it hid the alarm that swept over him at the thought of what he and Jenny had still to do. The black whetstone had to be found and it could be in a ditch or a rubbish dump ... anywhere.

But there had to be a clue. Surely there was something in what Old Cottle had said that would lead somewhere. However, only doubts crowded his mind as Kit stepped on the ice in the village to skate to town. The day was dreary, the snow was soft and wet and clogged his blades, and there was nothing outstanding in the way he moved. It was an ordinary skater who looked up at the row of houses along the riverside and saw the post office where his mother was now behind the counter. Its shop window was rimmed with coloured lights so that it stood out like a bright stamp on a drab envelope. It seemed to contain all the pleasures that were forbidden him. He slogged his way into town.

The Cake Shop Café was at last beginning to catch up with the Christmas season, but there was still work

89

to be done and he and Jenny were sent to tidy the kitchen. It was where her father would be working when the cafe reopened and it was almost ready for him to take over, but Jenny's mind was not on her work. The whetstone ... it had to be found, but neither she nor Kit had any idea where to start. And then her father came in carrying a bundle.

'Make way, you two,' he said and put his burden down on the long kitchen counter they had been cleaning. Then he caught sight of his daughter's expression and held up his hands. 'Nothing to do with me,' he said cheerfully. 'I'm only carrying out orders from your grandfather ... these bits and bobs are his idea to give the place a bit of atmosphere – a touch of the fens.'

'It looks like a bunch of garden tools,' said Kit.

'Not far off.' Jenny's father picked up a strangely shaped spade. 'This is used for slicing peat out in the fens, and that sickle is for cutting reeds for thatch.'

Kit picked up an iron shaft with five jagged spikes at one end.

'And that's an eel prong – a kind of spear for catching eels.'

'Makes me shudder,' said Jenny.

'Sharp, too,' her father told her. 'They're all going to be pinned to the wall when your grandfather gets round to it.'

'But now,' Jenny complained, 'you've messed up this surface that we've just been cleaning!'

'Can't be helped, my girl.' He was still cheerful. 'When Tom Townsend sets his mind on something it's got to be done. So watch they don't cut your fingers.'

She was impatiently wiping the cupboards and the fronts of the drawers under the counter, and when one of the drawers stuck she threw her cloth down. It may have been to distract her father but, at that moment, Kit found himself picking up the reed cutter's sickle and saying, 'Sharp, did you say?'

'Very. You know what Tom Townsend is like – if a thing's got an edge on it he's got to keep it keen.'

At that moment Jenny lost all interest in cleaning the counter and turned to look at Kit. Their eyes met and held. They each knew what they must do. It took a whetstone to keep edges sharp ... and Tom Townsend had made sure the old fen tools were well polished.

Jenny turned to her father. 'Do you think that Granny would give us lunch?' she asked.

Before her father could speak, a voice answered from the open door, 'I heard that.' Tom Townsend had come to the head of the stairs. 'Come and have a bite with us – both of you.'

TWELVE

THE WHETSTONE

Tom Townsend's invitation to lunch had come too quickly. They walked on opposite sides of him as they trudged along slushy pavements towards Wilberforce Avenue. Kit and Jenny had only a vague idea of how they could find out what they needed to know.

'You don't have to worry about a thaw,' said Tom Townsend, pointing to the fen runners slung over Kit's shoulder. 'It's going to freeze again tonight ... and more snow's on the way.'

'We just can't be sure when we want to go skating

again,' said Jenny, looking around her grandfather to Kit. 'But it's likely to be pretty soon.'

'Yes,' Kit agreed.

'Tonight?'

'Maybe not, it all depends.'

Tom Townsend interrupted. 'Depends on what?'

'Well we may need some more equipment,' said Kit. 'Some little thing that we absolutely have to have before we set out.'

Jenny knew that by mentioning 'equipment' he meant the stone. 'Exactly!' she cried. 'And that's why we've got to follow every clue. Haven't we, Kit?'

'Yes,' he agreed, but what clue she seemed to be hinting at he did not know.

Her grandfather was amused. 'You two mystify me,' he said, and Kit also felt he himself was being left in the dark. He remained puzzled all through lunch.

They had finished eating when Jenny said to her grandfather, 'You certainly kept your old fen runners well polished – the blades really shine.' She glanced briefly at Kit, then away.

'That man,' said her grandmother, 'is far too keen on sharpening things.'

'There's nothing like a nice keen edge if you've got work to do, Connie.'

Kit saw Jenny lean forward, but she deliberately did not catch his eye.

Connie went on, 'It's an obsession with you, Tom. You remember that time a few years ago, just before we closed the shop, when things were going wrong at the café and everyone there was very unhappy and talking about the strange atmosphere there seemed to be everywhere in the building – when that was going on you used to spend half your time in your workshop cleaning things, polishing them up?' It was obviously an old disagreement between them, and she suddenly smiled at the other two. 'But those times are long gone, and you are both helping us put it all behind us.'

Jenny glanced at Kit to get his attention and then spoke carefully to her grandfather. 'The blades on our skates have a very keen edge – what did you use to sharpen them?'

She heard Kit draw in his breath. Perhaps she was being too obvious, but now Tom Townsend was answering her.

'Oh, I used any of the usual things ... they're all there on my workbench.'

Jenny's coaxing had come to nothing. They had been in Tom Townsend's workshop and there had been no black whetstone on his bench.

'Nothing in particular,' he repeated, 'just the usual things.'

'Except,' his wife said, 'there was that lump of black rock you used to go on about because you said it was so very good.'

'Oh that!' He was laughing. 'My precious whetstone!'

The electricity that leapt between Kit and Jenny must have been obvious, but they did not even glance at each other, and Connie went on, 'What on earth became of it?'

He shrugged. 'I must have lost it.'

Kit and Jenny risked looking at each other. But disappointment at her grandfather's remark silenced them both.

Jenny made a last attempt. 'But surely it's somewhere here. Where have you looked?'

'Everywhere.'

'Where did you get it?'

He laughed. 'You want to know a lot! But I'm afraid I can't remember.'

Connie broke in. 'Oh yes, you can, Tom! You just want to forget it, that's all. And you may well look sheepish.' She turned to her granddaughter. 'It was that time he fell through the ice – when he behaved so stupidly under the bridge. It was in the mud at the water's edge, wasn't it, Tom?'

'Now that you've reminded me of my foolishness, Connie, I do remember. I used it to scrape mud off my skate and I kept it.'

'Goodness knows why,' said Connie, 'but now you've lost it.'

'Afraid so, and it's definitely not in my workshop.'

'How can you be so certain?' Jenny asked.

'Because years ago I took it to the café and we used it in the kitchen.'

Kit and Jenny cried out together, 'So you *do* know where it is!'

Tom Townsend grimaced. 'Sorry,' he said. 'We did use it in the café kitchen for a time – and we had the sharpest kitchen knives in town, but then it vanished . . . melted clean away. Probably thrown out with the rubbish . . . gone for ever.'

But they could still make one last search, and they were in the hall putting on their coats when the phone rang and Tom Townsend went to answer it. He came back in a hurry. 'No more skating for you today, Kit – that was Jenny's mother. She's worried because there's a real storm brewing and they think the roads will soon be blocked – so off you go and catch the last bus out of town!'

Kit and Jenny looked at each other. They both knew that their last chance of finding the whetstone lay in the café.

'Tomorrow,' he muttered as they parted. 'We'll look for it tomorrow.' They had no choice. It was impossible to get to Cottle's Bridge tonight.

THIRTEEN

A TATTERED HEDGE

It was a slow journey. Kit was near enough to the bus driver to see him crouched over his wheel to peer beyond the swish of his wiper blades into the darkness. The banks of whiteness on the verges were already joined in the middle of the highway.

'And it's freezing again,' said the driver. 'This is a one-way trip for me tonight, I reckon – no return journey.'

Kit stepped off into a silent village. 'That church and them trees,' said the driver, 'make it one big Christmas card – watch how you go.' And when the bus had gone Kit was left thinking that each soft flake was pulling sound out of the air and muffling it in the humped hedgerows.

In the Back of Beyond snow hugged his feet and he was alone until he saw a curtain pulled aside at the window of Mrs Strickland's cottage and a moment later she came stepping down the path, hugging herself against the cold and calling his name.

'Christopher, I'm so glad you're home – was the journey terribly bad?' She gave him no time to answer but went on, 'Someone came to see you . . . just before it got dark.'

'Who was it?' he asked unnecessarily because she immediately went on.

'It was a very old man, and he should never have been out on a night like this, as I told him, but he said – quite politely, I must say – that neither snow nor cold troubled him, and I imagine it didn't because he did seem very well wrapped up . . . but Kit, he wanted to see you . . . have you any idea who he might be?'

Kit did know, but he did not say. There were secrets he must not give away. 'Did he tell you what he wanted?' he asked.

'Well, hardly.' Mrs Strickland had a shawl over her head but was already having to wipe snowflakes from her glasses. 'He spoke very clearly for such a very old man, but all I could make out was that he expected you to be going somewhere … and *tonight* of all nights, which of course is utter nonsense.'

'Tonight?' Kit could not believe what she was saying. Already the snow was ankle-deep on the ice and more was falling, but even if they did make an attempt they would have nothing to take with them. They had not yet found the whetstone. He stepped closer to Mrs Strickland. 'What else did he say? Did he mention anything about what we should bring with us?'

'His mind was wandering, Kit. He didn't make sense. But he said over and over that you would find the *blizzard track* and he would be waiting.'

'Nothing else?'

'Nothing, Kit. Can you please tell me what this is all about? That poor old man was in a bad way.'

'I met him once,' Kit admitted. 'He says strange things.'

'And now he's coming to you for help.' She was full of sympathy.

'How long ago did this happen?' Kit asked.

'Only minutes. He said he'd wait. I'm surprised you didn't see him at the end of the lane.'

Kit was already turning away. 'I'll see if I can find him.'

Snow topped the hedgerow and was thick on the

verge. He came to the end of the lane where it joined the road and the hedge ceased. There was no traffic and no Old Cottle to tell him more. He turned to go back, and as he did so he saw that at one place in the hedge the snow seemed shadowed and clotted thicker than elsewhere. He stepped closer. A rag, blown there by the wind some time ago, hung among the twigs. He brushed snow away. More rags, rags he felt he recognised. Layers of rags were caught up in the twigs and the remnants of a tattered cap had snow frozen to its peak.

He looked for footprints. There were none. Even the ruts left by the car when his father had come home had filled in and were barely visible.

The breeze was increasing and snowflakes were blinding him as he searched for a message in the rags, but there was nothing. The rags themselves were the message. And tonight he and Jenny had to act.

Kit crouched in the lee of the hedge. Old Cottle had vanished, but he had left instructions. Jenny must be told – everything depended on her. She had to find the whetstone. He thought no further than that. Find the stone. He had to tell her but it was impossible to get into town. No traffic was passing through the village. He took out his mobile phone. It was useless to try to speak to her directly, she had not been able to free herself from the screeching she heard whenever she put a phone to her ear, and even if there had been a change and she could hear him she could not possibly do alone what he was to ask. Joe could help. Kit made the call.

FOURTEEN

TOUCHING THE STONE

Jenny, in her room at the top of the house, gazed out over the rooftops. The town was hunched under its thick white blanket, and the moon gazed down from a clear sky. Nothing stirred, but her mind was restless. She knew where the whetstone lay. She was sure of it. It could be nowhere else. So why had she not made an excuse to go back to the café instead of allowing herself to be hurried home while Kit caught his bus? Now the stone had to lie unguarded in the darkness while other seekers roamed the night.

When she heard Joe's voice in the hall below she

knew something else had gone wrong. Her heart was beating so strongly when she went to the head of the stairs that she had to grip the handrail to steady herself as she gazed down.

'Kit rang me,' Joe was saying, 'and it sounded urgent.'

Her mother said something that Jenny did not catch, and then Joe's voice again: 'Kit told me he was locked out for a while when he got home because he'd left his keys in the café.' Joe laughed at that, and then her mother asked, 'But why on earth didn't he ring me instead of calling you out on a night like this?'

'He felt a bit of a fool, I suppose . . . and he thought it would save you the trouble if I went to the café with Jenny. She would know where he left them. It would put his mind at rest.' Joe was still amused.

Her mother was saying that her husband would go later when he got home but by that time Jenny was in the hall. 'I'll go with Joe right now.' She was breathless, already seeking her coat. 'I know Kit's worried about his keys.'

And Joe, acting mischievously, added, 'And I'll take care of her, Mrs Townsend.'

'See you do.' She herself was beginning to think Kit's fussiness was amusing.

Outside, their heads bent into the freezing air,

Jenny said, 'It wasn't the keys, was it? It was something else.'

His hood was pulled forward too far for her to see his face but she heard him say, 'I don't know what it is with you two, but he did say to tell you that you had to find a stone, of all the stupid things, and you had to find it tonight ... he kept saying *tonight* as if that was almost the most important thing of all.'

They had come to the café and were standing in front of the cake shop window on the ground floor. Jenny shielded her eyes as she pressed her face close to the glass. Nothing moved within the shop.

'I know you two like to pretend you see things that I can't, but do you see anything there?' Joe asked.

'No.' she said. 'Not at the moment.'

'I'm cold,' he said, 'and I'm wondering why I'm here. If it wasn't so close to Christmas I wouldn't be playing games like this. So what's so important about this stone?'

'It is ancient.' She had drawn back and watched the vapour that came from her mouth as she formed the words. Words made visible in the air. A sort of spell. She would tell Joe everything he wanted to know. 'It was stolen and has to be returned.'

'Where?'

'Dutchman's Cut.' She was leaning forward to unlock the door as she spoke.

'Why?' he said as they stepped inside.

'Because the old man you saw out there says so.'

'Old Cottle ...? I might have known.' Joe was amused, but now they were climbing the dark stairs, and when they got to the top he pressed a switch but no lights came on. Another snag. Jenny had forgotten they had been disconnected while some work was done, but when they stepped into the cafe enough light came through the great arched window facing the street to show the tables and chairs already set out and waiting for customers.

He followed her through the swing doors into the kitchen and almost bumped into her in the dimness when she stopped. He began to whisper, asking a question, and he saw her raise her hand for silence as they stood together, looking and listening.

Joe could imagine figures forming in the grainy darkness but he allowed himself a snort to let her know this was an empty room and when dawn came it would have shed all its mystery. She advanced a slow step and they became grey ghosts drifting towards a long counter beneath which Joe could just make out rows of cupboards and drawers.

Jenny paused. 'Wait,' she whispered. The counter top should have been clear, but something lay there. She went forward so cautiously that she caused Joe to feel that something was watching them. Then the edge of his hood touched his cheek like a thin finger and he started back just as Jenny turned towards him. 'False alarm,' she said softly. The clutter was no more than the old objects from the fens that her grandfather was to put on display.

She moved closer to the counter. It was difficult in the dimness to make out the drawers underneath until she crouched and could run her fingers along their edges. The shadow along the edge of one drawer showed slightly thicker than the others.

'It won't close properly,' she whispered. 'There's something behind it.'

This was her only clue. She had noticed it earlier. The whetstone must have been used on this counter to sharpen knives and at some time it had fallen to the back of the drawer and been forgotten.

Joe watched as she crouched and pulled gently at the drawer's handle. It did not move easily and he found himself gazing around the silent room to protect her back as she tensed herself and pulled harder. She caught her breath but the drawer moved silently and she knelt in front of it and reached inside.

Jenny's fingers were cold but she could feel the texture of the wood and, as if her fingertips had eyes, she saw in her mind the back of the drawer and then its top edge. She bent her wrist to reach into the space behind it and touched a narrow ledge in the woodwork. Her fingers worked along it. There was dust, and she felt her fingers leaving a trail as she slid them slowly along its length. Nothing. She reached deeper and her fingers moved as delicately as a spider until they halted at the touch of something cold and as smooth as water. She believed she could even feel its blackness as her fingertips edged behind the whetstone.

Joe heard her draw in her breath at the same moment that he caught a glimpse of movement in the far corner of the room. He jerked forward and snatched up an iron rod that lay on the counter. As he raised it he was aware that it was a many-pointed spear and he swung round with it just as a tall figure emerged from the corner.

He was not aware of Jenny's gasp as the stone slid from her fingers, but the clatter as it fell behind the drawer made him shuffle back towards her as the tall figure angled itself clear of the shadows and stepped closer.

Jenny hauled at a lower drawer. It shot out too easily and she lost her balance and fell to the floor alongside it. She could not tell if the whetstone had fallen within it and she was sweeping inside it with both hands. Joe, unbalanced by his lunge, was on his knees. They were helpless in the empty room waiting for the dark figure to stride forward and look down on them. They heard their own unsteady breathing but no other sound. Apart from themselves the room seemed empty.

Joe was the first to stir. Then Jenny, and slowly they got to their feet. Joe held his spear ready to jab again, but no figure emerged from the shadows.

Together they touched the stone. 'It's not very big,' said Joe. 'Hardly seems worth the trouble,' and suddenly they were both laughing. 'I really thought something was coming towards me,' he said, 'but I was just jabbing this stupid spear into nothing.'

Jenny knew she was laughing too much. 'You did look a bit weird,' she said. Joe had no idea what had really happened and she knew she could never convince him. 'But you were very brave,' she told him, and she meant it.

'Let's get out of here,' he said.

He took the eel spear with him. 'It's a bit too heavy for you,' he said, and she allowed him to think so. She carried the sickle that had once been used for cutting reeds out in the fens. 'You can't be too careful on the way home,' he said, happily playing along with the game he believed she and Kit were imagining.

The wind had picked up when they stepped outside and snow was blowing horizontally along the street '... which reminds me,' said Joe. 'Kit told me to tell you, several times, that you would both meet on the *blizzard track*, whatever that means. Well, it looks as though you've got the blizzard but there's not much track that I can see.' Market Street was already filled with snow to pavement level. 'It's a pity you won't be able to see him tonight as he seemed to expect.'

She was still puzzling over what Kit's words meant when they got back to the Crescent, but panic drove it out of her mind when her mother asked if they had found Kit's keys.

Once again Joe saved her. 'Kit lives in a daze,' he said. 'He'll find them in his pocket.'

'I suppose so,' Jenny agreed, but she could not meet Joe's eye.

FIFTEEN

THE BLIZZARD TRACK

Jenny did not sleep. The smooth black whetstone had never left her. It was twice the length of her palm, heavy and slender, easy to conceal inside her coat, and safe now under her pillow.

She put her fingertips to it as if to understand the black silkiness within it and guessed at its urge to touch steel. Long ago it had been swept along the edge of a sword blade to make it gleam, and now she knew that in her grandfather's hands it had touched knives in the café kitchen. Before he lost it he had taken pleasure in brightening the jagged tips of the eel spear with which Joe had held back the Watcher in the dark shadows of the café. And she could imagine the smile on Tom Townsend's face as he had smoothed the edge of the fen runners before handing them to Kit. The same had happened to the skate boots that now lay beside her bed. But the time had come for the stone to be returned to Fendyke Pool far out across the fens.

Beneath the warmth of her duvet she thought for a moment of the snow that lay thick on rooftops and so deeply muffled the town that now, past midnight, no traffic ran. Then, in the silent house, she slid out of bed, dressed quickly, and padded quietly downstairs. As she huddled in her coat in the hall she caught a glimpse of the reed cutter's sickle that lay beside the doormat where she had left it. That, too, had felt the touch of the stone. She picked it up.

Snow had drifted against the front door and it came over the tops of her rubber boots as she stepped outside, but the wind itself had dropped. Walking was difficult until she reached the narrow alleyways leading to the canal but on its banks she suddenly realised that skating would be impossible. The canal was pure white from bank to bank and the tears she felt on her cheeks were not caused by the cold.

She would fail. The whole calm night was indifferent to her. The snow was thick and only her desperation forced her to flounder down the bank, throw off her boots and lace up her skates.

She took an awkward step. She would walk and then she would crawl and if she froze and could go no further that was how Kit would find her.

But she still had the reed-cutter's sickle. She lunged at the snow with it but its tip struck ice and jarred her wrist. She struck again. The ice in the centre of the canal was just beneath the surface of the snow – and it was then that she remembered the words that Kit had made Joe repeat to her '. . . Kit told me to tell you . . . the *blizzard track*!'

She thrust a foot forward. Under a mere skim of snow her blade ran on pure ice. High winds, channelled down the centre of the canal, had cleared a way for her. She had found the blizzard track.

The dim lights of the path alongside the canal were soon behind her and her eyes were getting used to the darkness of the open country when she saw, some distance ahead, an upright shadow standing in the very centre of the canal. She slewed to a standstill. Even at this distance the rasp of her skates must have been heard in the stillness of the night, yet the figure did not move. Her mind leapt to the dark figure in the gloom of the cafe. She withdrew the sickle from beneath her anorak and slid silently forward.

She halted again when the dark figure raised an arm and she held herself ready for an attack, but then a voice came clearly on the night air, calling her name. She advanced slowly. The voice could be a trap luring her into danger. Once again she slid to a standstill, and waited.

The mist of her breath clouded her vision and she was raising her weapon higher when the figure came gliding closer, calling her name, and a moment later it was Kit who stood there and at first held out a hand to her but then opened his arms and held her close.

'I've been waiting a long time,' he said. 'I was afraid you wouldn't understand Joe's message.'

Her face was pressed into the cold material of his shoulder. 'I've got the stone,' she said quietly. Theirs were the only two voices. The whole night appeared to be listening.

They separated and stood side by side gazing out into the darkness. He saw the sickle in her hand and she told him that at some time the whetstone must have touched it. Kit took it. 'You are the one to carry the stone,' he said. 'I am only your guard.'

His village was crouched under deep snow with only dark windows gazing at them as they sped through on the blizzard track not caring who heard the rasp and glide of each long stride. Then out into the open fenland just as more snow came floating on the still air and pressed around them in curtains that thickened and cut them off from everything except the utter loneliness.

In the narrow waterways the blizzard track was filling up and became more difficult to follow but still Kit pressed on with clogged skates until a sudden swirl of snow blinded him.

Jenny came alongside him. They both looked towards the sky. Thick cloud hid the moon and stars. There was nothing but the ghostly light of the snow, and darkness.

Kit saw the glimmer of her face but could not make out her expression even with his head close to hers. 'There's only one thing I know,' he said. 'We must be close to Dutchman's Cut.' It was guesswork. He knew that the high bank of the cut crossed the flat landscape from horizon to horizon, but his sense of direction had deserted him.

She watched him wipe snow from the sickle as he lifted his head and tried to sense which way they should travel, and a sudden doubt stabbed her mind. The whetstone. She could not feel its weight in her pocket. It must somehow have worked free as she stumbled in the narrow channels. She threw off a glove and plunged her hand inside her coat. She could feel the stone's hardness in the lining but she had to touch it to be sure. Her fingers closed over it, but as she was about to speak to Kit she saw him turn his head away as if he had seen something.

She looked in the same direction but saw only barren snow. Then she realised he was not looking. His head was tilted and he was listening. She, too, tilted her head and after a moment, from far away, she heard thin, sharp cries that seemed for an instant like the voices of children, but then Kit spoke.

'Birds,' he said. 'Something has disturbed them.'

He knew of a place where water birds were fed in winter but had not imagined they were so close. He listened again. The cries were faint and confused, but he was certain he heard birds quarrelling over food – and that could mean that somewhere ahead there was a patch of open water.

'Dutchman's Cut can't be far away,' he said, and she followed him along a narrow channel that wound its way across the flat land until, quite suddenly, he was helping her out of the ditch and they were digging their skates sideways into a steep bank of snow and then sliding in an avalanche down towards the ice on the other side.

'The blizzard track!' he shouted. 'It's there again.'

A roadway of black ice broad enough for them to skate side by side cut through the whiteness and disappeared into the distance. But there were no birds even though the air was full of feathery snowflakes that whirled and spun with them as their skates ran forward, now as silent as oil.

'Two miles to go!' Kit leant into the darkness, sensing his swiftness by the scrolls of spiralling snow he was making as he cut through the air. Jenny lagged slightly behind and he glanced over his shoulder to see that she, too, was making the snow writhe in spinning clouds around her.

He was about to forge further ahead and clear a path for her when a thin tendril of snow brushed his cheek and held for a moment. He brushed it aside but then another touched his shoulder and clung. He twisted clear but as he sped along more white tendrils reached for him and then he saw that thin human shapes were tiptoeing along the ice, keeping pace and gazing at him with huge hollow eyes.

He leant into a turn that had his fingertips dragging the ice but all the time he felt the tendrils whipping and clinging and slowing him down.

The full turn brought him behind Jenny but before he could catch up with her the air was full of the whickering thin shrieks he had mistaken for birds. The skinny limbs of snow wraiths had trapped their prey and Jenny was surrounded and about to be dragged down.

Kit had the sickle in his hand. It was his only weapon, but the whetstone had been used on it and its edge was eager to do damage. He heard it whistle as it sliced air then felt the luscious sharpness as it cut into white limbs and left them writhing on the ice. Then a head fell, startled and useless, and he was a warrior circling the girl who was of far more value than himself, and he hacked and conquered and followed her as she sped free along the straight black road of ice.

The bridge, when it came, was bare. There was no ragged man waiting to welcome them, and as they clung together in the shadow of the span, fighting to regain their breath, they began to realise there was yet another barrier between them and Fendyke Pool below them at the bottom of Dutchman's Cut.

The ice was solid from bank to bank, a foot thick and as hard as rock.

SIXTEEN

OUT OF REACH

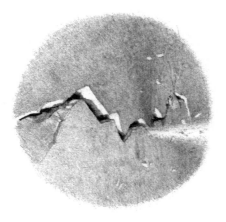

Winter had locked them out of the secret depths of Dutchman's Cut. Even in the shelter of the bridge where normally there would have been some seepage of water at the edges the ice was welded to the bank. They stamped on it but it did nothing except jar their ankles, and when Kit took the reed cutter's sickle and hacked at the ice where it seemed to be weakest the scratch was barely visible. Fendyke Pool, where Jenny must drop the whetstone, was out of reach.

It was at that moment that the whole night chose to mock them. The clouds thinned so that the moon let them see they were no more than two tiny beetles, pinpricks of shadow in a gaping white wilderness where nothing moved.

Jenny glanced down. The well was directly beneath her feet. Suddenly she crouched, took out the black whetstone and brought it down with all her force on the black ice. Nothing shattered. She beat on it again but her effort was no more than a faint rapping in the night and at last she stood up, gasping and defeated.

She glanced at Kit, but he was paying her no attention. He was looking back along Dutchman's Cut to where the channel was lost in the distance. She saw nothing and was about to speak when Kit reached out and grasped her hand. His grip hurt and she was struggling to free her fingers when she saw a change in the ice road that had brought them here. In the distance, silently, a slab of ice tore itself free of the banks, tilted upwards until it stood vertically, lost its balance, broke into fragments and fell.

It was then that the thunder of its fall came rolling towards them, filling the sky, and as it died away they saw, lying on the unbroken ice, a dark shape. It could have been a heap of black mud vomited up from the depths but the moon gave it a silvery gleam that Kit remembered with a jolt of fear. He and Joe had seen that same silvery glimmer slip through the water under Cottle's Bridge. And now he saw what lay on the ice.

It was a huge head, as flat-topped as a snake's with a slot of a mouth that opened and hung like a black pouch big enough to swallow a cow.

Panic locked their limbs and they stood and watched when, as if to haul itself clear, the Longlode Worm reached forward with one long, clawed foot but, before the rest of its body was out of the water, the ice split under its weight and a long crack sped like an arrow to the tips of their skates. Even at that moment Jenny hesitated. If the crack opened a shade wider she could drop the whetstone through to the bottom of Dutchman's Cut. With Kit alongside her she was bending forward to do it when pressure from the advancing dragon tilted the ice beneath them, jammed the crack tight and sprayed them with water from the depths.

They fled. Their skates moved with agonising perfection over the glassy road and they kept ahead of the Worm with ease but with every stroke they were further from the ancient well where the stone must be dropped. They paused to look back. To leave the ice and hope to get back along the bank was an impossibility. On land the worm could move much faster than they could run. And now, as they watched, they saw the gaping head rise even higher and Cottle's Bridge smash into fragments and be hurled aside while the beast ploughed the frozen channel into jagged ice floes. They turned away. They could do nothing more than keep clear of the mouth and claws.

Kit had been drenched when the ice split. He wiped his face, tasting the water on his lips. Stupidly, in the midst of all that was happening, he was aware that he was thirsty and he wanted to drink.

Jenny saw him lick the water drops from the back of his hand and he was skating so slowly he seemed to have lost all hope. Even worse, he slowed until he was at a standstill. She was reaching to urge him on when he suddenly flung back his head and yelled, 'Fresh water!'

The moon showed her Kit's pale face and eyes that glinted with madness as he shouted at the sky, 'Dutchman's Cut is fresh water!'

Jenny felt tears on her face. He had lost all hope and now, in a frenzy, he was pointing ahead and crying out, 'The sea is that way!'

The great beast was coming faster. Mountains of ice were heaved aside and crashed into the banks, but Kit was reaching for Jenny's hand to pull her closer as they fled before it. 'Old Cottle told us it came from the sea.' They had slowed and his voice was gasping but no longer mad and their faces were close together. 'But the Longlode Worm grew huge in the pure water of the fens . . . do you remember?'

She nodded.

'*So now salt water is its enemy!*'

A new crack came arrowing towards them and the ice tilted. Kit sprawled and Jenny saved him, but now he was dragging her to the bank and they climbed frantically to the top. On the other side the flat land opened out to a horizon already showing faintly grey as the sun rose and so dead level that it could only have been water. They had fled towards the coast and the sea was in sight.

Neither spoke. They slid down the bank on to a frozen marsh. Crooked runs of frozen mud ran between patches of snow and grass, and they were skating where they could, then stumbling and running when the ice ran out and their skates cut into frozen sand. They stumbled and fell. Kit wrenched off his boots and skates. Jenny did the same. Behind them was the grinding roar as the Worm thrashed through the ice. In front of them grass merged with a wide beach and the sea's edge. He pointed further along the shore to where a wooden breakwater jutted out from the beach into deep water.

'We run for that!' he cried.

Jenny took the stone from her pocket and they flung off everything that could drag them down before they fled barefoot and almost naked through the grass. They stumbled as they reached the soft sand while behind them the last mass of ice came crashing down the bank and the beast reared its head against the sky.

They did not see it slide down the bank and begin its writhing lizard walk across the marsh.

They were heading at an angle across the beach towards the breakwater but the soft sand was making them stumble. 'The sea!' Kit gasped and they changed direction until they were running directly for the water's edge. It was there, on the cold wet sand that they ran faster.

Behind them was an ominous silence and it was Kit again who snatched a glance over his shoulder to see that the monster was heading to cut them off. He risked losing the last of his breath to gasp, 'Get into deeper water . . . you have the stone!'

He stumbled and fell. She stooped to help him, but he waved her off and pointed to the wooden posts that jutted from the sand. She looked back. It was as though a foul river had been released onto the sand and a black torrent was writhing towards them. She ran, splashing through the wavelets of the calm sea, and reached the first of the wooden posts and climbed on the heavy beam that reached out into deeper water. Her feet slipped on matted seaweed but she reached the second post and then out to the next where the slow waves of the sullen sea climbed and clung as if to push her back and she had to dig her nails into the slippery wood and could go no further. Helplessly she looked back.

'Jenny!' She heard Kit's voice but saw nothing until the small figure at the water's edge raised an arm and his voice came again, 'Show it the stone!'

Kit had the sickle in his hand. It was useless and he knew it. The beast had reached the water's edge and its clawed feet were already splashing through the shallows. It had no fear of the sea.

Jenny saw the pale dawn sky glint on its scales as her frozen fingers clawed at the whetstone in her pocket and held it above her head. It was pitifully useless. The beast along the shore was even larger than it had seemed in Dutchman's Cut. Its jaw sprang open above her and its tail thrashed the sea to sweep Kit aside and leave him battered and defeated on the sand.

As darkness cascaded down on her Jenny flung herself from the breakwater into the hollow of a black wave. Kit caught one glimpse of her in the water before the jaw came down and she was lost. He ran towards where she had disappeared. He had the sickle. He would hack until he found her.

He was waist deep when one huge lizard eye swivelled towards him. It was out of reach but the beast had spotted him. He waded deeper and as he did so the head rolled away from him and Jenny broke out of the suck of the sea and staggered towards him.

They backed away. The salt sea water had finally done its work. The great head lay slackly on the waves and its dead eyes saw nothing.

They dragged themselves to the beach and stood in the surf. Jenny could barely hold herself upright. Her head was bowed. 'I've lost the stone,' she said, but when Kit tried to hold her hand he found that her fingers still clasped it, and all along the shore, like glittering foam at the water's edge, lay the scaly skin of the Longlode Worm.

Afterwards they remembered how painful it was to get skates on to frozen feet and fumble to dress with icy fingers. But they discovered there was enough unbroken ice at the edge of Dutchman's Cut to take them back to Cottle's Bridge. Its shattered remains jutted out of a patch of clear water that was on the verge of freezing over when Jenny cleared a space and let the black whetstone sink out of sight

They stood back, waiting for a sign, but none came. When they moved away the whisper of their skates dissolved in the white silence.

SEVENTEEN

A STRANGER

Kit woke to find his clothes almost dry on the radiator in his room. There was no need to explain anything to anyone. He would never be believed.

'About time you surfaced,' said his father when Kit got downstairs for breakfast. 'They've got the snow-ploughs out early and if you're thinking of going into town there's a bus in twenty minutes.'

'I'll skate.'

'You won't – the river's blocked solid all the way into town.'

His mother joined in. 'You could stay at home and help me.'

'Ha!' His father laughed at that. 'His girlfriend wants to see him.'

'No, she doesn't.' Kit's words came out too quickly.

'Leave the boy alone.' His mother tried to rescue him. 'Can't you see you've made him blush?'

'Don't forget I've seen her,' said his father. 'Well worth a blush I'd say.'

So much snow had blown against her window while she slept that Jenny woke in a dimness that made her believe it was still night. Even her mother's voice, calling to her, seemed far away.

She turned over, snuggling deeper into the warmth of her duvet, but as she did so a bright corner opened in her mind and suddenly she remembered. Damp clothes hung over a chair where she had left them. She thrust them under her bed and went downstairs.

Her mother's eyes were on her. 'You're looking very tired, Jenny.'

'Bad dream, Mum.' Crashing ice was in her head. A nightmare. 'I was being chased.'

'Are you sure that your grandfather really needs you at the cafe this morning?'

Jenny could see by her mother's face that she was worried that Jenny was once more seeing things invisible to anyone else. 'I'd really like to be there today, Mum . . . there's still a lot to do before the big opening.'

Her mother became mischievous. 'I don't suppose that boy will be there, will he? There's been a lot of snow overnight.'

Jenny shook her head. So much that could never have happened was still in her mind. She had to thrust it all away. She remembered skating with Kit in the night, and that may have happened, but all else was a dream. And now it was all fading. She was free.

Her mother had gone through into the hall. 'I don't know how it could have happened, Jenny, but your boots are half full of snow.'

From the window of the bus Kit saw that the river was choked with snow but there was no sign of a blizzard track. He was tired, he closed his eyes, and the swaying of the bus was rocking him to sleep when a man in the seat behind him said, 'I didn't hear nothin' last night.'

'Nor did I,' said a woman, 'but I spoke to a man who came in from Weldelph this morning and he said that the whole of Dutchman's Cut was shook up by an earth tremor and the ice was all churned up and one of them old bridges was shattered to bits.'

'And that's not all,' said another voice from further along the bus. 'Something was washed up from the sea and lay all silvery along the shore. Beautiful sight, they say.'

Joe had already heard about it when Kit got to the café and Jenny, pale faced, was listening to him, but saying nothing. It was all over. There had simply been a storm in the night which had disturbed them as they slept. They were exhausted and worked so silently as the big room became a great glittering cave that Joe became impatient with them. He left them alone and went to make an improvement to the tree standing in the centre of the big window overlooking the street. His back was turned when Jenny took something from her pocket and laid it on the table in front of Kit.

Her voice was little more than a whisper. 'I wonder if I'll need this any more,' she said.

It was her charm bracelet. They both could see the pearly gleam of the dragon scale. Neither spoke. They both knew what she would do and she reached forward and gripped the scale firmly enough between her thumb and forefinger to lift the heavy bracelet from the table. There was a faint rattle from the charms and they both turned their heads to gaze around the room.

They peered into the dim corners but nowhere was there a tall shadow with a long head tilted their way. The Watcher had gone.

It was at that moment that Joe, standing at the

window, turned towards them and said, 'I think we have visitors.'

Jenny, in a panic, ran to the window sure that she would be haunted by a dark figure standing in the snow. Suddenly she was laughing. 'It's my grandparents – but who's that with them?'

There was another couple, and now it was Kit's turn to put her mind at rest. 'One of them is my neighbour,' he said, and it was Mrs Strickland who climbed the stairs with the others and took over the conversation as soon as she entered the room.

'Christopher,' she said to Kit, 'I have been intending to see Connie and Tom ever since you reminded me about that episode when poor Tom went through the ice and I was just standing out there alone looking up at this huge window . . . and it really did look like a great grotto with all its coloured lights . . . when this gentleman came up to me.' She turned to the stranger, who bowed, '. . . and you will never guess who it is!'

She did not give them time to answer. 'He's the young man who came to our aid that day when we had to rescue poor Tom!'

'Not so young now,' said the man. He was not tall, but he was bulky under his overcoat.

'He's Mister . . .' she turned to him '. . . oh I'm so sorry but I didn't catch your name.'

The man, however, had spotted their skates under

the table and he picked up the fen runners. 'And these, if I am not mistaken, are the very skates you were using that day, Tom?'

'Afraid so,' Tom Townsend confessed. 'They've both been to the bottom under Cottle's Bridge.'

The man was running his thumb along the blades. 'You've kept a good edge on them, Tom,' and he picked up Jenny's skate boots. 'And these must belong to the young maid.' He bowed to her, taking off his cap. There was a broad smile on his red, weather-beaten face. He touched the blades again. 'I should think there's at least one more good outing for them before Tom's magic wears off.'

Then he was gone before anyone could say anything to stop him.

'Just like the last time,' said Mrs Strickland. 'And he's left his cap.'

The Cake Shop Café was crowded that night and no one noticed when Jenny and Kit slipped out into the freezing darkness. The canal was deserted and the only sound was the whisper of their skates as they found the blizzard track, and next morning the only sign they had been as far as Cottle's Bridge was a cap left hanging on a broken handrail.